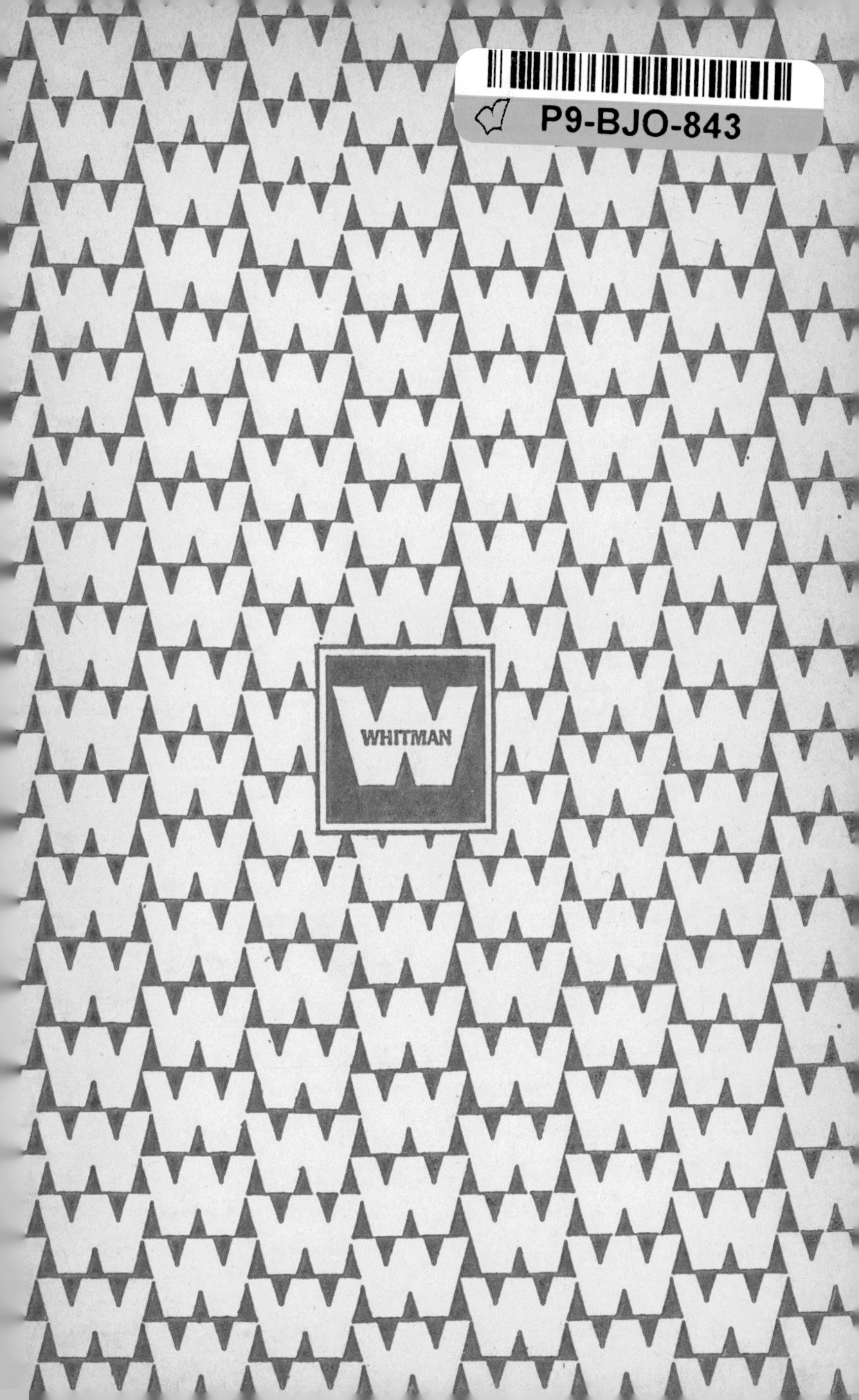
P9-BJO-843
WHITMAN

tales of
EDGAR ALLAN POE

ELEVEN BIZARRE STORIES
From the Master Teller of Tales

ILLUSTRATED BY

Jerry E. Johnson

A WHITMAN BOOK
Western Publishing Company, Inc.
Racine, Wisconsin

CONTENTS

The Cask of Amontillado

THE THOUSAND INJURIES of Fortunato I had borne as I best could, but when he ventured upon insult, I vowed revenge. You, who so well know the nature of my soul, will not suppose, however, that I gave utterance to a threat. *At length* I would be avenged; this point was definitively settled—but the very definitiveness with which it was resolved precluded the idea of risk. I must not only punish but punish with impunity. A wrong is unredressed when retribution overtakes its redresser. It is equally unredressed when the avenger fails to make himself felt as such to him who has done the wrong.

It must be understood that neither by word nor deed had I given Fortunato cause to doubt my goodwill. I continued, as was my wont, to smile in his face, and he did not perceive that my smile *now* was at the thought of his immolation.

He had a weak point, this Fortunato, although in other regards he was a man to be respected and even feared. He prided himself on his connoisseurship in wine. Few Italians have the true virtuoso spirit. For the most part, their enthusiasm is adopted to suit the time and opportunity to practice imposture upon the British and Austrian *millionaires.* In painting and gemmary, Fortunato, like his countrymen, was a quack, but in the matter of old wines he was sincere. In this respect I did not differ from him materially; I was skillful in the Italian vintages myself and bought largely whenever I could.

It was about dusk one evening during the supreme madness of the carnival season that I encountered my friend. He accosted me with excessive warmth, for he had been drinking much. The man wore motley. He had on a tight-fitting, parti-striped dress, and his head was surmounted by the conical cap and bells. I was so pleased to see him that I thought I should never have done wringing his hand.

I said to him, "My dear Fortunato, you are luckily met. How remarkably well you are looking today! But I have received a pipe of what passes for amontillado, and I have my doubts."

"How?" said he. "Amontillado? A pipe? Impossible! And in the middle of the carnival?"

"I have my doubts," I replied, "and I was silly enough to pay the full amontillado price without consulting you in the matter. You were not to be found, and I was fearful of losing a bargain."

"Amontillado!"

"I have my doubts."

"Amontillado!"

"And I must satisfy them."

"Amontillado!"

"As you are engaged, I am on my way to Luchesi. If anyone has a critical turn, surely it is he. Luchesi will tell me—"

"Luchesi cannot tell amontillado from sherry."

"And yet some fools will have it that his taste is a match for your own."

"Come, let us go."

"Whither?"

"To your vaults."

"My friend, no; I will not impose upon your good nature. I perceive you have an engagement. Luchesi—"

"I have no engagement; come."

"My friend, no. It is not the engagement but the severe cold with which I perceive you are afflicted. The vaults are insufferably damp. They are encrusted with niter."

"Let us go, nevertheless. The cold is merely nothing. Amontillado! You have been imposed upon; and as for Luchesi, he cannot distinguish sherry from amontillado."

Thus speaking, Fortunato possessed himself of my arm. Putting on a mask of black silk and drawing a roquelaure closely about my person, I suffered him to hurry me to my *palazzo*.

There were no attendants at home; they had absconded to make merry in honor of the time. I had told them that I should not return until the morning and had given them explicit orders not to stir from the house. These orders were sufficient, I well knew, to insure their immediate disappearance, one and all, as soon as my back was turned.

I took from their sconces two flambeaux and, giving one to Fortunato, bowed him through several suites of rooms to the archway that led into the vaults. I passed down a long and winding staircase, requesting him to be cautious as he followed. We came at length to the foot of the descent and stood together on the damp ground of the catacombs of the Montresors.

The gait of my friend was unsteady, and the bells upon his cap jingled as he strode.

"The pipe," said he.

"It is farther on," said I, "but observe the white webwork which gleams from these cavern walls."

He turned toward me and looked into my eyes with

two filmy orbs that distilled the rheum of intoxication.

"Niter?" he asked, at length.

"Niter," I replied. "How long have you had that cough?"

"Ugh! ugh! ugh!—ugh! ugh! ugh!—ugh! ugh! ugh!—ugh! ugh! ugh!—ugh! ugh! ugh!"

My poor friend found it impossible to reply for many minutes.

"It is nothing," he said at last.

"Come," I said with decision, "we will go back; your health is precious. You are rich, respected, admired, beloved; you are happy, as once I was. You are a man to be missed. For me it is no matter. We will go back; you will be ill, and I cannot be responsible. Besides, there is Luchesi—"

"Enough," he said. "The cough is a mere nothing; it will not kill me. I shall not die of a cough."

"True—true," I replied, "and indeed I had no intention of alarming you unnecessarily—but you should use all proper caution. A draft of this Médoc will defend us from the damps."

Here I knocked off the neck of a bottle which I drew from a long row of its fellows that lay upon the mold.

"Drink," I said, presenting him the wine.

He raised it to his lips with a leer. He paused and nodded to me familiarly, while his bells jingled.

"I drink," he said, "to the buried that repose around us."

"And I to your long life."

He again took my arm, and we proceeded.

"These vaults," he said, "are extensive."

"The Montresors," I replied, "were a great and numerous family."

"I forget your arms."

"A huge human foot d'or, in a field azure; the foot crushes a serpent rampant, whose fangs are embedded in the heel."

"And the motto?"

*"Nemo me impune lacessit."**

"Good!" he said.

The wine sparkled in his eyes, and the bells jingled. My own fancy grew warm with the Médoc. We had passed through walls of piled bones, with casks and puncheons intermingling, into the inmost recesses of the catacombs. I paused again, and this time I made bold to seize Fortunato by an arm, above the elbow.

"The niter!" I said. "See, it increases. It hangs like moss upon the vaults. We are below the river's bed. The drops of moisture trickle among the bones. Come, we will go back ere it is too late. Your cough—"

"It is nothing," he said. "Let us go on. But first another draft of the Médoc."

I broke and reached him a flagon of De Grave. He emptied it at a breath. His eyes flashed with a fierce light. He laughed and threw the bottle upward with a gesticulation I did not understand.

I looked at him in surprise. He repeated the movement —a grotesque one.

"You do not comprehend?" he said.

"Not I," I replied.

"Then you are not of the brotherhood."

"How?"

"You are not of the masons."

"Yes, yes," I said, "yes, yes."

"You? Impossible! A mason?"

"A mason," I replied.

"A sign," he said.

---

*"No one injures me without being punished."

"It is this," I answered, producing a trowel from beneath the folds of my roquelaure.

"You jest!" he exclaimed, recoiling a few paces. "But let us proceed to the amontillado."

"Be it so," I said, replacing the tool beneath the cloak and again offering him my arm. He leaned upon it heavily. We continued our route in search of the amontillado. We passed through a range of low arches, descended, passed on, and, descending again, arrived at a deep crypt, in which the foulness of the air caused our flambeaux rather to glow than flame.

At the most remote end of the crypt there appeared another, less spacious. Its walls had been lined with human remains piled to the vault overhead, in the fashion of the great catacombs of Paris. Three sides of this interior crypt were still ornamented in this manner. From the fourth, the bones had been thrown down and lay promiscuously upon the earth, forming at one point a mound of some size. Within the wall thus exposed by the displacing of the bones, we perceived a still interior recess, in depth about four feet, in width three, in height six or seven. It seemed to have been constructed for no especial use in itself but formed merely the interval between two of the colossal supports of the roof of the catacombs and was backed by one of their circumscribing walls of solid granite.

It was in vain that Fortunato, uplifting his dull torch, endeavored to pry into the depths of the recess. Its termination the feeble light did not enable us to see.

"Proceed," I said. "Herein is the amontillado. As for Luchesi—"

"He is an ignoramus," interrupted my friend as he stepped unsteadily forward, while I followed immediately at his heels. In an instant he had reached the extremity of

the niche and, finding his progress arrested by the rock, stood stupidly bewildered. A moment more and I had fettered him to the granite. In its surface were two iron staples, distant from each other about two feet horizontally. From one of these depended a short chain, from the other a padlock. Throwing the links about his waist, it was but the work of a few seconds to secure it. He was too much astounded to resist. Withdrawing the key, I stepped back from the recess.

"Pass your hand," I said, "over the wall; you cannot help feeling the niter. Indeed it is *very* damp. Once more let me *implore* you to return. No? Then I must positively leave you. But I must first render you all the little attentions in my power."

"The amontillado!" ejaculated my friend, not yet recovered from his astonishment.

"True," I replied. "The amontillado."

As I said these words, I busied myself among the pile of bones of which I have before spoken. Throwing them aside, I soon uncovered a quantity of building stone and mortar. With these materials and with the aid of my trowel, I began vigorously to wall up the entrance of the niche.

I had scarcely laid the first tier of my masonry when I discovered that the intoxication of Fortunato had in a great measure worn off. The earliest indication I had of this was a low, moaning cry from the depth of the recess. It was *not* the cry of a drunken man. There was then a long and obstinate silence. I laid the second tier, and the third, and the fourth; and then I heard the furious vibrations of the chain. The noise lasted for several minutes, during which, that I might hearken to it with the more satisfaction, I ceased my labors and sat down upon the bones. When at last the clanking subsided, I resumed the trowel and finished, without interruption, the fifth, the sixth, and the seventh tiers. The wall was now nearly upon a level with my breast. I again paused and, holding the flambeaux over the masonwork, threw a few feeble rays upon the figure within.

A succession of loud and shrill screams, bursting suddenly from the throat of the chained form, seemed to thrust me violently back. For a brief moment I hesitated —I trembled. Unsheathing my rapier, I began to grope with it about the recess, but the thought of an instant reassured me. I placed my hand upon the solid fabric of the catacombs and felt satisfied. I reapproached the wall. I replied to the yells of him who clamored. I reechoed—I aided—I surpassed them in volume and in strength. I did this, and the clamorer grew still.

It was now midnight, and my task was drawing to a close. I had completed the eighth, the ninth, and the tenth tiers. I had finished a portion of the eleventh and the last; there remained but a single stone to be fitted and plastered in. I struggled with its weight; I placed it partially in its destined position. But now there came from the niche a low laugh that erected the hairs upon my head. It was succeeded by a sad voice, which I had difficulty in recognizing as that of the noble Fortunato. The voice said, "Ha! ha! ha!—he! he!—a very good joke indeed—an excellent jest. We will have many a rich laugh about it at the *palazzo*—he! he! he!—over our wine—he! he! he!"

"The amontillado!" I said.

"He! he! he!—he! he! he!—yes, the amontillado. But is it not getting late? Will not they be awaiting us at the *palazzo*, the Lady Fortunato and the rest? Let us be gone."

"Yes," I said, "let us be gone."

"For the love of God, Montresor!"

"Yes," I said, "for the love of God!"

But to these words I hearkened in vain for a reply. I grew impatient. I called aloud, "Fortunato!"

No answer. I called again: "Fortunato!"

No answer still. I thrust a torch through the remaining aperture and let it fall within. There came forth in return only a jingling of the bells. My heart grew sick—on account of the dampness of the catacombs. I hastened to make an end of my labor. I forced the last stone into its position; I plastered it up. Against the new masonry I reerected the old rampart of bones. For the half of a century, no mortal has disturbed them.

In pace
*requiescat!**

---

*"Rest in peace."

The Black Cat

For the most wild, yet most homely, narrative which I am about to pen, I neither expect nor solicit belief. Mad indeed would I be to expect it in a case where my very senses reject their own evidence. Yet mad am I not—and very surely do I not dream. But tomorrow I die, and today I would unburden my soul. My immediate purpose is to place before the world, plainly, succinctly, and without comment, a series of mere household events. In their consequences, these events have terrified—have tortured—have destroyed me. Yet I will not attempt to expound them. To me they have presented little but horror—to many they will seem less terrible than *baroques*. Hereafter, perhaps, some intellect may be found which will reduce my phantasm to the commonplace—some intellect more calm, more logical, and far less excitable than my own, which will perceive, in the circumstances I detail with awe, nothing more than an ordinary succession of very natural causes and effects.

From my infancy I was noted for the docility and humanity of my disposition. My tenderness of heart was even so conspicuous as to make me the jest of my companions. I was especially fond of animals and was indulged by my parents with a great variety of pets. With these I spent most of my time and never was so happy as when feeding and caressing them. This peculiarity of character grew with my growth, and in my manhood I derived from it one of my principal sources of pleasure. To those who have cherished an affection for a faithful and sagacious dog, I need hardly be at the trouble of explaining the nature or the intensity of the gratification thus derivable. There is something in the unselfish and self-sacrificing love of a brute which goes directly to the heart of him who has had frequent occasion to test the paltry friendship and gossamer fidelity of mere *man*.

I married early and was happy to find in my wife a disposition not uncongenial with my own. Observing my partiality for domestic pets, she lost no opportunity of procuring those of the most agreeable kind. We had birds, goldfish, a fine dog, rabbits, a small monkey, and *a cat*.

This latter was a remarkably large and beautiful animal, entirely black and sagacious to an astonishing degree. In speaking of his intelligence, my wife, who at heart was not a little tinctured with superstition, made frequent allusion to the ancient popular notion which regarded all black cats as witches in disguise. Not that she was ever *serious* upon this point, and I mention the matter at all for no better reason than that it happens just now to be remembered.

Pluto—this was the cat's name—was my favorite pet and playmate. I alone fed him, and he attended me wherever I went about the house. It was even with difficulty that I could prevent him from following me through the streets.

Our friendship lasted in this manner for several years, during which my general temperament and character—through the instrumentality of the fiend Intemperance—had (I blush to confess it) experienced a radical alteration for the worse. I grew, day by day, more moody, more irritable, more regardless of the feelings of others. I suffered myself to use intemperate language to my wife. At length, I even offered her personal violence. My pets, of course, were made to feel the change in my disposition. I not only neglected but also ill-used them. For Pluto, however, I still retained sufficient regard to restrain me from maltreating him, as I made no scruple of maltreating the rabbits, the monkey, or even the dog, when by accident or through affection they came in my way. But my disease grew upon me—for what disease is like alcohol!—and at length even Pluto, who was now becoming old and consequently somewhat peevish—even Pluto began to experience the effects of my ill temper.

One night, returning home much intoxicated from one of my haunts about town, I fancied that the cat avoided my presence. I seized him, when, in his fright at my violence, he inflicted a slight wound upon my hand with his teeth. The fury of a demon instantly possessed me. I knew myself no longer. My original soul seemed at once to take its flight from my body, and a more than fiendish malevolence, gin nurtured, thrilled every fiber of my frame. I took from my waistcoat pocket a penknife, opened it, grasped the poor beast by the throat, and deliberately cut one of its eyes from the socket! I blush, I burn, I shudder while I pen the damnable atrocity.

When reason returned with the morning—when I had slept off the fumes of the night's debauch—I experienced a sentiment half of horror, half of remorse, for the crime of which I had been guilty, but it was at best a feeble and equivocal feeling, and the soul remained untouched. I again plunged into excess and soon drowned in wine all memory of the deed.

In the meantime the cat slowly recovered. The socket of the lost eye presented, it is true, a frightful appearance, but he no longer appeared to be suffering any pain. He went about the house as usual but, as might be expected, fled in extreme terror at my approach. I had so much of my old heart left as to be at first grieved by this evident dislike on the part of a creature which had once so loved me. But this feeling soon gave place to irritation. And then came, as if to my final and irrevocable overthrow, the spirit of *perverseness.* Of this spirit, philosophy takes no account. Yet I am not more sure that my soul lives than I am that perverseness is one of the primitive impulses of the human heart—one of the indivisible primary faculties or sentiments which gave direction to the character of man. Who has not, a hundred times, found himself committing a vile or a silly action for no other reason than that he knows he should *not?* Have we not a perpetual inclination, in the teeth of our best judgment, to violate that which is *law,* merely because we understand it to be such? This spirit of perverseness, I say, came to my final overthrow. It was this unfathomable longing of the soul *to vex itself*—to offer violence to its own nature—to do wrong for the wrong's sake only—that urged me to continue and finally to consummate the injury I had inflicted upon the unoffending brute. One morning, in cold blood, I slipped a noose about its neck and hung it to the limb of a tree; hung it with the tears streaming from my eyes and with the bitterest remorse at my heart; hung it *because* I knew that it had loved me and *because* it had given me no reason of offense; hung it *because* I knew that in so doing I was committing a sin—a deadly sin that would so jeopardize my immortal soul as to place it, if such a thing were possible, even beyond the reach of the infinite mercy of the Most Merciful and Most Terrible God.

On the night of the day on which this cruel deed was done, I was aroused from sleep by the cry of fire. The curtains of my bed were in flames. The whole house was blazing. It was with great difficulty that my wife, a servant, and I made our escape from the conflagration. The destruction was complete. My entire worldly wealth was swallowed up, and I resigned myself thenceforward to despair.

I am above the weakness of seeking to establish a sequence of cause and effect between the disaster and the atrocity. But I am detailing a chain of facts and wish not to leave even a possible link imperfect. On the day succeeding the fire, I visited the ruins. The walls, with one exception, had fallen in. This exception was found in a compartment wall, not very thick, which stood about the middle of the house, against which had rested the head of my bed. The plastering had here in great measure resisted the action of the fire, a fact which I attributed to its having been recently spread. About this wall a dense crowd were collected, and many persons seemed to be examining a particular portion of it with very minute and eager attention. The words "Strange!" "Singular!" and other similar expressions excited my curiosity. I approached and saw, as if graven in bas-relief upon the white surface, the figure of a gigantic *cat*. The impression was given with an accuracy truly marvelous. There was a rope about the animal's neck.

When I first beheld this apparition—for I could scarcely regard it as less—my wonder and my terror were extreme. But at length reflection came to my aid. The cat, I remembered, had been hung in a garden adjacent to the house. Upon the alarm of fire, this garden had been immediately filled by the crowd, by some one of whom the animal must have been cut from the tree and thrown through an open window into my chamber. This had probably been done with the view of arousing me from sleep. The falling of other walls had compressed the victim of my cruelty into the substance of the freshly spread plaster, the lime of which, with the flames and the ammonia from the carcass, had then accomplished the portraiture as I saw it.

Although I thus readily accounted to my reason, if not altogether to my conscience, for the startling fact just detailed, it did not the less fail to make a deep impression upon my fancy. For months I could not rid myself of the phantasm of the cat, and during this period there came back into my spirit a half sentiment that seemed, but was not, remorse. I went so far as to regret the loss of the animal and to look about me among the vile haunts which I now habitually frequented for another pet of the same species and of somewhat similar appearance, with which to supply its place.

One night, as I sat half stupefied in a den of more than infamy, my attention was suddenly drawn to some black object reposing upon the head of one of the immense hogsheads of gin or of rum which constituted the chief furniture of the apartment. I had been looking steadily at the top of this hogshead for some minutes, and what now caused me surprise was the fact that I had not sooner perceived the object thereupon. I approached it and touched it with my hand. It was a black cat—a very large one, fully as large as Pluto and closely resembling him in every respect but one. Pluto had not a white hair upon any portion of his body, but this cat had a large, although indefinite, splotch of white, covering nearly the whole region of the breast.

Upon my touching him, he immediately arose, purred loudly, rubbed against my hand, and appeared delighted with my notice. This, then, was the very creature of which I was in search. I at once offered to purchase it from the landlord, but this person made no claim to it—knew nothing of it—had never seen it before.

I continued my caresses, and when I prepared to go home, the animal evinced a disposition to accompany me. I permitted it to do so, occasionally stooping and patting it as I proceeded. When it reached the house, it domesticated itself at once and became immediately a great favorite with my wife.

For my own part, I soon found a dislike to it arising within me. This was just the reverse of what I had anticipated, but—I know not how or why it was—its evident fondness for me rather disgusted and annoyed me. By slow degrees these feelings of disgust and annoyance rose into the bitterness of hatred. I avoided the creature, a certain sense of shame and the remembrance of my former deed of cruelty preventing me from physically abusing it. I did not, for some weeks, strike or otherwise violently ill-use it, but gradually—very gradually—I came to look upon it with unutterable loathing and to flee silently from its odious presence as one cringes from the breath of a pestilence.

What added, no doubt, to my hatred of the beast was the discovery, on the morning after I brought it home, that, like Pluto, it also had been deprived of one of its eyes. This circumstance, however, only endeared it to my wife, who, as I have already said, possessed in a high degree that humanity of feeling which had once been my distinguishing trait and the source of many of my simplest and purest pleasures.

With my aversion to this cat, however, its partiality to me seemed to increase. It followed my footsteps with a pertinacity which it would be difficult to make the reader comprehend. Whenever I sat, it would crouch beneath my chair or spring upon my knees, covering me with its loathsome caresses. If I arose to walk, it would get between my feet and thus nearly throw me down or, fastening its long and sharp claws in my dress, clamber in this manner to my breast. At such times, although I longed to destroy it with a blow, I was yet withheld from so doing, partly by a memory of my former crime, but chiefly—let me confess it at once—by absolute *dread* of the beast.

This dread was not exactly a dread of physical evil—and yet I should be at a loss how otherwise to define it. I am almost ashamed to own—yes, even in this felon's cell, I am almost ashamed to own it—that the terror and horror with which the animal inspired me had been heightened by one of the merest chimeras it would be possible to conceive. My wife had called my attention more than once to the character of the mark of white hair of which I have spoken, which constituted the sole visible difference between the strange beast and the one I had destroyed. The reader will remember that this mark, although large, had been originally very indefinite, but by slow degrees—degrees nearly imperceptible, which for a long time my reason struggled to reject as fanciful—it had at length assumed a rigorous distinctness of outline. It was now the representation of an object that I shudder to name—and for this, above all, I loathed and dreaded it and would have rid myself of the monster *had I dared*—it was now, I say, the image of a hideous—of a ghastly thing—of the *gallows!*—O mournful and terrible engine of horror and of crime—of agony and of death!

And now was I indeed wretched beyond the wretchedness of mere humanity. And *a brute beast*—whose fellow I had contemptuously destroyed—*a brute beast*—to work out for *me*—for me, a man, fashioned in the image of the High God—so much of insufferable woe! Alas! Neither by day nor by night knew I the blessing of rest anymore!

During the former, the creature left me no moment alone; and in the latter, I started hourly from dreams of unutterable fear, to find the hot breath of *the thing* upon my face and its vast weight—an incarnate nightmare that I had no power to shake off—incumbent eternally upon my *heart!*

Beneath the pressure of torments such as these, the feeble remnant of the good within me succumbed. Evil thoughts became my sole intimates—the darkest and most evil of thoughts. The moodiness of my usual temper increased to hatred of all things and of all mankind, while from the sudden frequent and ungovernable outbursts of a fury to which I now blindly abandoned myself, my uncomplaining wife, alas, was the most usual and the most patient of sufferers.

One day she accompanied me upon some household errand into the cellar of the old building which our poverty compelled us to inhabit. The cat followed me down the steep stairs and, nearly throwing me headlong, exasperated me to madness. Uplifting an ax and forgetting, in my wrath, the childish dread which had hitherto stayed my hand, I aimed a blow at the animal, which, of course, would have proved instantly fatal had it descended as I wished. But this blow was arrested by the hand of my wife. Goaded by the interference into a rage more than demoniacal, I withdrew my arm from her grasp and buried the ax in her brain. She fell dead upon the spot, without a groan.

This hideous murder accomplished, I set myself forthwith, with entire deliberation, to the task of concealing the body. I knew that I could not remove it from the house, either by day or by night, without the risk of being observed by the neighbors. Many projects entered my mind. At one period I thought of cutting the corpse into minute fragments and destroying them by fire. At another I resolved to dig a grave for it in the floor of the cellar. Again, I deliberated about casting it in the well in the yard—about packing it in a box, as if merchandise, with the usual arrangements, and so getting a porter to take it from the house. Finally I hit upon what I considered a far better expedient than either of these. I determined to wall it up in the cellar—as the monks of the middle ages are recorded to have walled up their victims.

For a purpose such as this, the cellar was well adapted. Its walls were loosely constructed and had lately been plastered throughout with a rough plaster, which the dampness of the atmosphere had prevented from hardening. Moreover, in one of the walls was a projection caused by a false chimney or fireplace that had been filled up and made to resemble the rest of the cellar. I made no doubt that I could readily displace the bricks at this point, insert the corpse, and wall the whole up as before, so that no eye could detect anything suspicious.

And in this calculation I was not deceived. By means of a crowbar, I easily dislodged the bricks, and, having carefully deposited the body against the inner wall, I propped it in that position, while with little trouble I relaid the whole structure as it originally stood. Having procured mortar, sand, and hair with every possible precaution, I prepared a plaster which could not be distinguished from the old, and with this I very carefully went over the new brickwork. When I had finished, I felt satisfied that all was right. The wall did not present the slightest appearance of having been disturbed. The rubbish on the floor was picked up with the minutest care. I looked around triumphantly and said to myself, "Here at last, then, my labor has not been in vain."

My next step was to look for the beast which had been

the cause of so much wretchedness, for I had at length firmly resolved to put it to death. Had I been able to meet with it at the moment, there could have been no doubt of its fate, but it appeared that the crafty animal had been alarmed at the violence of my previous anger and forebore to present itself to me in my present mood. It is impossible to describe or to imagine the deep, the blissful, sense of relief which the absence of the detested creature occasioned in my bosom. It did not make its appearance during the night—and thus for one night, at least, since its introduction into the house, I soundly and tranquilly slept—aye, *slept,* even with the burden of murder upon my soul!

The second and the third day passed, and still my tormentor came not. Once again I breathed as a free man. The monster, in terror, had fled the premises forever! I should behold it no more! My happiness was supreme! The guilt of my dark deed disturbed me but little. Some few inquiries had been made, but these had been readily answered. Even a search had been instituted—but of course nothing was to be discovered. I looked upon my future felicity as secured.

Upon the fourth day following the assassination, a party of the police came very unexpectedly into the house and proceeded again to make a rigorous investigation of the premises. Secure, however, in the inscrutability of my place of concealment, I felt no embarrassment whatever. The officers bade me accompany them in their search. They left no nook or corner unexplored. At length, for the third time, they descended into the cellar. I quivered not in a muscle. My heart beat as calmly as that of one who slumbers in innocence. I walked the cellar from end to end. I folded my arms upon my bosom and roamed easily to and fro. The police were thoroughly satisfied and prepared to depart. The glee at my heart was too strong to be restrained. I burned to say if but one word by way of triumph and to render doubly sure their assurance of my guiltlessness.

"Gentlemen," I said at last, as the party ascended the steps, "I delight to have allayed your suspicions. I wish you all health—and a little more courtesy. By the by, gentlemen, this—this is a very well-constructed house." (In the rabid desire to say something easily, I scarcely knew what I uttered at all.) "I may say, an *excellently* well-constructed house. These walls—are you going, gentlemen?—these walls are solidly put together." And here, through the mere frenzy of bravado, I rapped heavily with a cane which I held in my hand upon that very portion of the brickwork behind which stood the corpse of the wife of my bosom.

But may God shield and deliver me from the fangs of the archfiend! No sooner had the reverberation of my blows sunk into silence than I was answered by a voice from within the tomb!—by a cry, at first muffled and broken, like the sobbing of a child, and then quickly swelling into one long, loud, and continuous scream, utterly anomalous and inhuman—a howl—a wailing shriek, half of horror and half of triumph, such as might have arisen only out of hell, conjointly from the throats of the damned, in their eternal agony, and of the demons that exult in the damnation.

Of my own thoughts it is folly to speak. Swooning, I staggered to the opposite wall. For one instant the party upon the stairs remained motionless, through extremity of terror and of awe. In the next a dozen stout arms were toiling at the wall. It fell bodily. The corpse, already greatly decayed and clotted with gore, stood erect before the eyes of the spectators. Upon its head, with red extended mouth and solitary eye of fire, sat the hideous beast whose craft had seduced me into murder and whose informing voice had consigned me to the hangman. I had walled the monster up within the tomb!

The Telltale Heart

TRUE! NERVOUS, very, very dreadfully nervous, I had been and am; but why *will* you say that I am mad? The disease had sharpened my senses, not destroyed, not dulled them. Above all was the sense of hearing acute. I heard all things in the heaven and in the earth. I heard many things in hell. How, then, am I mad? Hearken! And observe how healthily, how calmly, I can tell you the whole story.

It is impossible to say how first the idea entered my brain, but, once conceived, it haunted me day and night. Object there was none. Passion there was none. I loved the old man. He had never wronged me. He had never given me insult. For his gold I had no desire. I think it was his eye! Yes, it was this! One of his eyes resembled that of a vulture—a pale blue eye with a film over it. Whenever it fell upon me, my blood ran cold, and so, by degrees, very gradually, I made up my mind to take the life of the old man and thus rid myself of the eye forever.

Now, this is the point. You fancy me mad. Madmen know nothing. But you should have seen *me*. You should have seen how wisely I proceeded—with what caution, with what foresight, with what dissimulation I went to work! I was never kinder to the old man than during the whole week before I killed him. And every night about midnight, I turned the latch of his door and opened it—

oh, so gently! And then, when I had made an opening sufficient for my head, I put in a dark lantern, all closed, closed so that no light shone out, and then I thrust in my head. Oh, you would have laughed to see how cunningly I thrust it in! I moved it slowly, very, very slowly, so that I might not disturb the old man's sleep. It took me an hour to place my whole head within the opening so far that I could see him as he lay upon his bed. Ha! Would a madman have been so wise as this? And then, when my head was well in the room, I undid the lantern cautiously—oh, so cautiously—cautiously (for the hinges creaked) I undid it just so much that a single thin ray fell upon the vulture eye. And this I did for seven long nights, every night just at midnight, but I found the eye always closed, and so it was impossible to do the work, for it was not the old man who vexed me but his *evil eye*. And every morning, when the day broke, I went boldly into the chamber and spoke courageously to him, calling him by name in a hearty tone and inquiring how he had passed the night. So, you see, he would have been a very profound old man, indeed, to suspect that every night, just at twelve, I looked in upon him while he slept.

Upon the eighth night I was more than usually cautious in opening the door. A watch's minute hand moves more quickly than did mine. Never before that night had I *felt* the extent of my own powers, of my sagacity. I could scarcely contain my feelings of triumph. To think that there I was, opening the door little by little, and he not even to dream of my secret deeds or thoughts. I fairly chuckled at the idea, and perhaps he heard me, for he moved on the bed suddenly, as if startled. Now, you may think that I drew back—but no. His room was as black as pitch with the thick darkness (for the shutters were close fastened through fear of robbers), and so I knew that he could not see the opening of the door, and I kept pushing it on steadily, steadily.

I had my head in and was about to open the lantern, when my thumb slipped upon the tin fastening, and the old man sprang up in the bed, crying out, "Who's there?"

I kept quite still and said nothing. For a whole hour I did not move a muscle, and in the meantime I did not hear him lie down. He was still sitting up in the bed, listening, just as I have done night after night, hearkening to the deathwatches in the wall.

Presently I heard a slight groan, and I knew it was the groan of mortal terror. It was not a groan of pain or of grief—oh, no! It was the low, stifled sound that arises from the bottom of the soul overcharged with awe. I knew this sound well. Many a night, just at midnight, when all the world slept, it has welled up from my own bosom, deepening, with its dreadful echo, the terrors that distracted me. I say I knew it well. I knew what the old man felt and pitied him, although I chuckled at heart. I knew that he had been lying awake ever since the first slight noise, when he had turned in the bed. His fears had been ever since growing upon him. He had been trying to fancy them causeless but could not. He had been saying to himself, "It is nothing but the wind in the chimney," "It is only a mouse crossing the floor," or "It is merely a cricket which has made a single chirp." Yes, he had been trying to comfort himself with these suppositions, but he had found all in vain. *All in vain,* because Death, in approaching him, had stalked with his black shadow before him and enveloped the victim. And it was the mournful influence of the unperceived shadow that caused him to feel—although he neither saw nor heard—to *feel* the presence of my head within the room.

When I had waited a long time, very patiently, without

hearing him lie down, I resolved to open a little—a very, very little—crevice in the lantern. So I opened it—you cannot imagine how stealthily, stealthily—until at length a single dim ray, like the thread of the spider, shot out from the crevice and fell upon the vulture eye.

It was open—wide, wide open—and I grew furious as I gazed upon it. I saw it with perfect distinctness—all a dull blue, with a hideous veil over it that chilled the very marrow in my bones, but I could see nothing else of the old man's face or person, for I had directed the ray, as if by instinct, precisely upon the damned spot.

And now have I not told you that what you mistake for madness is but overacuteness of the senses? Now, I say, there came to my ears a low, dull, quick sound, such as a watch makes when enveloped in cotton. I knew *that* sound well, too. It was the beating of the old man's heart. It increased my fury as the beating of a drum stimulates the soldier into courage.

But even yet I refrained and kept still. I scarcely breathed. I held the lantern motionless. I tried how steadily I could maintain the ray upon the eye. Meantime the hellish tattoo of the heart increased. It grew quicker and quicker and louder and louder every instant. The old man's terror *must* have been extreme! It grew louder, I say, louder every moment! Do you mark me well? I have told you that I am nervous. So I am. And now, at the dead hour of the night, amid the dreadful silence of that old house, so strange a noise as this excited me to uncontrollable terror. Yet, for some minutes longer, I refrained and stood still. But the beating grew louder, louder! I thought the heart must burst. And now a new anxiety seized me—the sound would be heard by a neighbor! The old man's hour had come! With a loud yell, I threw open the lantern and leaped into the room. He shrieked once

—once only. In an instant I dragged him to the floor and pulled the heavy bed over him. I then smiled gaily, to find the deed so far done. But for many minutes the heart beat on with a muffled sound. This, however, did not vex me; it would not be heard through the wall. At length it ceased. The old man was dead. I removed the bed and examined the corpse. Yes, he was stone, stone dead. I placed my hand upon the heart and held it there many minutes. There was no pulsation. He was stone dead. His eye would trouble me no more.

If still you think me mad, you will think so no longer when I describe the wise precautions I took for the concealment of the body. The night waned, and I worked hastily but in silence.

I took up three planks from the flooring of the chamber and deposited all between the scantlings. I then replaced the boards so cleverly, so cunningly, that no human eye—not even *his*—could have detected anything wrong. There was nothing to wash out—no stain of any kind—no blood spot whatever. I had been too wary for that.

When I had made an end of these labors, it was four o'clock—still as dark as midnight. As the bell sounded the hour, there came a knocking at the street door. I went down to open it with a light heart—for what had I *now* to fear? There entered three men who introduced themselves, with perfect suavity, as officers of the police. A shriek had been heard by a neighbor during the night; suspicion of foul play had been aroused; information had been lodged at the police office, and they (the officers) had been deputed to search the premises.

I smiled—for *what* had I to fear? I bade the gentlemen welcome. The shriek, I said, was my own in a dream. The old man, I mentioned, was absent, in the country. I took my visitors all over the house. I bade them search—search *well.* I led them, at length, to *his* chamber. I showed them his treasures, secure, undisturbed. In the enthusiasm of my confidence, I brought chairs into the room and desired them *here* to rest from their fatigues, while I myself, in the wild audacity of my perfect triumph, placed my own seat upon the very spot beneath which reposed the corpse of the victim.

The officers were satisfied. My *manner* had convinced them. I was singularly at ease. They sat, and while I answered cheerily, they chatted of familiar things. But, ere long, I felt myself getting pale and wished them gone. My head ached, and I fancied a ringing in my ears; but still they sat, and still they chatted. The ringing became more distinct; I talked more freely to get rid of the feeling, but it continued and gained definitiveness—until, at length, I found that the noise was *not* within my ears.

No doubt I now grew *very* pale, but I talked more fluently and with a heightened voice. Yet the sound increased—and what could I do? It was *a low, dull, quick sound—much such a sound as a watch makes when enveloped in cotton.* I gasped for breath, and yet the officers heard it not. I talked more quickly, more vehemently, but the noise steadily increased. I arose and argued about trifles in a high key and with violent gesticulations, but the noise steadily increased. Why *would* they not be gone? I paced the floor to and fro with heavy strides, as if excited to fury by the observations of the men, but the noise steadily increased. O God! What *could* I do? I foamed—I raved—I swore! I swung the chair upon which I had been sitting and grated it upon the boards, but the noise arose over all and continually increased. It grew louder—louder—*louder!* And still the men chatted pleasantly and smiled. Was it possible they heard not? Almighty God!—

no, no! They heard!—they suspected!—they *knew*—they were making a mockery of my horror! This I thought, and this I think. But anything was better than this agony! Anything was more tolerable than this derision! I could bear those hypocritical smiles no longer! I felt that I must scream or die! And now—again! Hark! Louder! Louder! Louder! *Louder!*

"Villains!" I shrieked. "Dissemble no more! I admit the deed! Tear up the planks! . . . Here, here! . . . It is the beating of his hideous heart!"

The Masque of the Red Death

THE "RED DEATH" had long devastated the country. No pestilence had ever been so fatal or so hideous. Blood was its avatar and its seal—the redness and the horror of blood. There were sharp pains and sudden dizziness, and then profuse bleeding at the pores, with dissolution. The scarlet stains upon the body, and especially upon the face of the victim, were the pest ban which shut him out from the aid and from the sympathy of his fellowmen; and the whole seizure, progress, and termination of the disease were the incidents of half an hour.

But the Prince Prospero was happy and dauntless and sagacious. When his dominions were half depopulated, he summoned to his presence a thousand hale and light-hearted friends from among the knights and dames of his court and, with these, retired to the deep seclusion of one of his castellated abbeys. This was an extensive and magnificent structure, the creation of the prince's own eccentric yet august taste. A strong and lofty wall girdled it in. This wall had gates of iron. The courtiers, having entered, brought furnaces and massy hammers and welded the bolts. They resolved to leave means neither of ingress nor of egress to the sudden impulses of despair from without or of frenzy from within. The abbey was amply provisioned. With such precautions, the courtiers might bid defiance to contagion. The external world could take care of itself. In the meantime, it was folly to grieve or to think. The prince had provided all the appliances of pleasure. There were buffoons, there were improvisatori, there were ballet dancers, there were musicians, there was beauty, there was wine. All these and security were within. Without was the Red Death.

It was toward the close of the fifth or sixth month of his seclusion and while the pestilence raged most furiously abroad that the Prince Prospero entertained his thousand friends at a masked ball of the most unusual magnificence.

It was a voluptuous scene, that masquerade. But first let me tell of the rooms in which it was held. There were seven—an imperial suite. In many palaces, however, such suites form a long and straight vista, while the folding doors slide back nearly to the walls on either hand, so that the view of the whole extent is scarcely impeded. Here the case was very different, as might have been expected from the duke's love of the bizarre. The apartments were so irregularly disposed that the vision embraced but little more than one at a time. There was a sharp turn at every twenty or thirty yards, and at each turn a novel effect. To the right and left, in the middle of each wall, a tall and narrow Gothic window looked out upon a closed corridor which pursued the windings of the suite. These windows were of stained glass, whose color varied in accordance with the prevailing hue of the decorations of the chamber into which it opened. That at the eastern extremity was hung, for example, in blue, and vividly blue were its windows. The second chamber was purple in its ornaments and tapestries, and here the panes were purple. The third was green throughout, and so were the casements. The fourth was furnished and lighted with orange, the fifth with white, the sixth with violet. The seventh apartment was closely shrouded in black velvet tapestries that hung all over the ceiling and down the walls, falling in heavy folds upon a carpet of the same material and hue. But, in this chamber only, the color of the windows failed to correspond with the decorations. The panes here were scarlet —a deep blood color. Now, in no one of the seven apartments was there any lamp or candelabrum amid the profusion of golden ornaments that lay scattered to and fro or depended from the roof. There was no light of any kind emanating from lamp or candle within the suite of chambers, but in the corridors that followed the suite, there stood opposite to each window a heavy tripod bearing a brazier of fire that projected its rays through the tinted glass and glaringly illumined the room. And thus were produced a multitude of gaudy and fantastic appearances. But in the western, or black, chamber, the effect of the firelight that streamed upon the dark hangings, through the blood-tinted panes, was ghastly in the extreme and produced so wild a look upon the countenances of those who entered that there were few of the company bold enough to set foot within its precincts at all.

It was in this apartment also that there stood against the western wall a gigantic clock of ebony. Its pendulum swung to and fro with a dull, heavy, monotonous clang; and when the minute hand made the circuit of the face, and the hour was to be stricken, there came from the brazen lungs of the clock a sound which was clear and loud and deep and exceedingly musical but of so peculiar a note and emphasis that, at each lapse of an hour, the musicians of the orchestra were constrained to pause momentarily in their performance to hearken to the sound; and thus the waltzers perforce ceased their evolutions, and there was a brief disconcert of the whole gay company, and while the chimes of the clock yet rang, it was observed that the giddiest grew pale, and the more aged and sedate passed their hands over their brows as if in confused reverie or meditation; but when the echoes had fully ceased, a light laughter at once pervaded the assembly; the musicians looked at each other and smiled, as if at their own nervousness and folly, and made whispering vows, each to the other, that the next chiming of the clock should produce in them no similar emotion, and then, after the lapse of sixty minutes (which embrace three thousand and six hundred seconds of the time that flies), there came yet another chiming of the clock, and then were the same disconcert and tremulousness and meditation as before.

But, in spite of these things, it was a gay and magnificent revel. The tastes of the duke were peculiar. He had a fine eye for colors and effects. He disregarded the decorum of mere fashion. His plans were bold and fiery, and his conceptions glowed with barbaric luster. There are some who would have thought him mad. His followers felt that he was not. It was necessary to hear and see and touch him to be *sure* that he was not.

He had directed, in great part, the movable embellishments of the seven chambers upon occasion of this great fete, and it was his own guiding taste which had given character to the masqueraders. Be sure, they were grotesque. There was much glare and glitter and piquancy and phantasm—much of what has been since seen in *Hernani*. There were arabesque figures with unsuited limbs and appointments. There were delirious fancies such as the madman fashions. There was much of the beautiful, much of the wanton, much of the bizarre, something of the terrible, and not a little of that which might have excited disgust. To and fro in the seven chambers there stalked, in fact, a multitude of dreams. And these —the dreams—writhed in and about, taking hue from the rooms and causing the wild music of the orchestra to seem as the echo of their steps. And anon there strikes the ebony clock which stands in the hall of the velvet, and then for a moment all is still and all is silent, save the voice of the clock. The dreams are stiff-frozen as they stand. But the echoes of the chime die away—they have endured but an instant—and a light, half-subdued laughter floats after them as they depart. And now again the music swells, and the dreams live and writhe to and fro more merrily than ever, taking hue from the many tinted windows through which stream the rays from the tripods. But to the chamber which lies most westwardly of the seven, there are now none of the maskers who venture; for the night is waning away; and there flows a ruddier light through the blood-colored panes; and the blackness of the sable drapery appalls; and to him whose foot falls upon the sable carpet, there comes from the near clock of ebony a muffled peal more solemnly emphatic than any which reaches *their* ears who indulge in the more remote gaieties of the other apartments.

But these other apartments were densely crowded, and in them beat feverishly the heart of life. And the revel went whirlingly on, until at length there commenced the sounding of midnight upon the clock. And then the music ceased, as I have told, and the evolutions of the waltzers were quieted, and there was an uneasy cessation of all things, as before. But now there were twelve strokes to be sounded by the bell of the clock, and thus it happened, perhaps, that more of thought crept, with more of time, into the meditations of the thoughtful among those who reveled. And thus, too, it happened, perhaps, that before the last echoes of the last chime had utterly sunk into silence, there were many individuals in the crowd who had found leisure to become aware of the presence of a masked figure which had arrested the attention of no single individual before. And the rumor of this new presence having spread itself whisperingly around, there arose at length from the whole company a buzz, or murmur, expressive of disapprobation and surprise—then finally of terror, of horror, and of disgust.

In an assembly of phantasms such as I have painted, it may well be supposed that no ordinary appearance could have excited such sensation. In truth, the masquerade license of the night was nearly unlimited, but the figure in question had out-Heroded Herod and gone beyond the bounds of even the prince's indefinite decorum. There are chords in the hearts of the most reckless which cannot be touched without emotion. Even with the utterly lost, to whom life and death are equally jests, there are matters of which no jest can be made. The whole company, indeed, seemed now deeply to feel that in the costume and bearing of the stranger neither wit nor propriety existed. The figure was tall and gaunt and shrouded from head to foot in the habiliments of the grave. The mask which concealed the visage was made so nearly to resemble the countenance of a stiffened corpse that the closest scrutiny must have had difficulty in detecting the cheat. And yet all this might have been endured, if not approved, by the mad revelers around. But the mummer had gone so far as to assume the type of the Red Death. His vesture was dabbled in *blood*—and his broad brow, with all the features of the face, was besprinkled with the scarlet horror.

When the eyes of Prince Prospero fell upon this spectral image (which, with a slow and solemn movement, as if more fully to sustain its role, stalked to and fro among the waltzers), he was seen to be convulsed in the first moment with a strong shudder, either of terror or distaste, but in the next his brow reddened with rage.

"Who dares—" he demanded hoarsely of the courtiers who stood near him, "who dares insult us with this blasphemous mockery? Seize him and unmask him, that we may know whom we have to hang at sunrise from the battlements!"

It was the eastern, or blue, chamber in which stood the Prince Prospero as he uttered these words. They rang throughout the seven rooms loudly and clearly—for the prince was a bold and robust man, and the music had become hushed at the waving of his hand.

It was the blue room where stood the prince, with a group of pale courtiers by his side. At first, as he spoke, there was a slight rushing movement of this group in the direction of the intruder, who, at the moment, was also near at hand, and now, with deliberate and stately step, made closer approach to the speaker. But, from a certain nameless awe with which the mad assumptions of the mummer had inspired the whole party, there were found none who put forth hand to seize him, so that, unimpeded, he passed within a yard of the prince's person; and while the vast assembly, as if with one impulse, shrank from the centers of the rooms to the walls, he made his way uninterruptedly, but with the same solemn and measured step which had distinguished him from the first, through the blue chamber to the purple—through the purple to the green—through the green to the orange—through this again to the white—and even thence to the violet, ere a decided movement had been made to arrest him. It was then, however, that the Prince Prospero, maddening with rage and the shame of his own momentary cowardice, rushed hurriedly through the six chambers, while none followed him, on account of a deadly terror that had seized upon all. He bore aloft a drawn dagger and had approached, in rapid impetuosity, to within three or four feet of the retreating figure, when the latter, having attained the extremity of the velvet apartment, turned suddenly and confronted his pursuer. There was a sharp cry —and the dagger dropped, gleaming, upon the sable carpet, upon which, instantly afterward, fell prostrate in death the Prince Prospero. Then, summoning the wild courage of despair, a throng of the revelers at once threw themselves into the black apartment and, seizing the mummer, whose tall figure stood erect and motionless within the shadow of the ebony clock, gasped in unutterable horror at finding the grave cerements and corpselike mask, which they handled with so violent a rudeness, untenanted by any tangible form.

And now was acknowledged the presence of the Red Death. He had come like a thief in the night; and one by one dropped the revelers in the blood-bedewed halls of their revel and died each in the despairing posture of his fall, and the life of the ebony clock went out with that of the last of the gay, and the flames of the tripods expired; and darkness and decay and the Red Death held illimitable dominion over all.

The Pit and the Pendulum

I WAS SICK, sick unto death, with that long agony, and when they at length unbound me and I was permitted to sit, I felt that my senses were leaving me. The sentence, the dread sentence of death, was the last of distinct accentuation which reached my ears. After that, the sound of the inquisitorial voices seemed merged into one dreamy, indeterminate hum. It conveyed to my soul the idea of *revolution,* perhaps from its association in fancy with the burr of a mill wheel. This only for a brief period, for presently I heard no more. Yet for a while I saw, but with how terrible an exaggeration! I saw the lips of the black-robed judges. They appeared to me white—whiter than the sheet upon which I trace these words—and thin even to grotesqueness; thin with the intensity of their expression of firmness, of immovable resolution, of stern contempt of human torture. I saw that the decrees of what to me was fate were still issuing from those lips. I saw them writhe with a deadly locution. I saw them fashion the syllables of my name, and I shuddered, because no sound succeeded. I saw, too, for a few moments of delirious horror, the soft and nearly imperceptible waving of the sable draperies which enwrapped the walls of the apartment; and then my vision fell upon the seven tall candles upon the table. At first they wore the aspect of charity and seemed white, slender angels who would save me. But then all at once there came a most deadly nausea over my spirit, and I felt every fiber in my frame thrill, as if I had touched the wire of a galvanic battery, while the angel forms became meaningless specters with heads of flame, and I saw that from them there would be no help. And then there stole into my fancy, like a rich musical note, the thought of what sweet rest there must be in the grave. The thought came gently and stealthily, and it seemed long before it attained full appreciation; but just as my spirit came at length properly to feel and entertain it, the figures of the judges vanished, as if magically, from before me; the tall candles sank into nothingness; their flames went out utterly; the blackness of darkness supervened; all sensations appeared swallowed up in a mad, rushing descent, as of the soul into Hades. Then silence and stillness and night were the universe.

I had swooned but still will not say that all of consciousness was lost. What of it there remained I will not attempt to define or even to describe; yet all was not lost. In the deepest slumber—no! In delirium—no! In a swoon—no! In death—no! Even in the grave, all *is not* lost, else there is no immortality for man. Arousing from the most profound of slumbers, we break the gossamer web of *some* dream. Yet, in a second afterward (so frail may that web have been), we remember not that we have dreamed. In the return to life from the swoon, there are two stages; first, that of the sense of mental or spiritual; second, that of the sense of physical existence. It seems probable that if, upon reaching the second stage, we could recall the impressions of the first, we should find these impressions eloquent in memories of the gulf beyond. And that gulf is—what? How at least shall we distinguish its shadows from those of the tomb? But if the impressions of what I have termed the first stage are not at will recalled, yet, after long interval, do they not come unbidden, while we marvel whence they come? He who has never swooned is not he who finds strange palaces and wildly familiar faces in coals that glow; is not he who beholds floating in midair the sad visions that the many may not view; is not he who ponders over the perfume of some novel flower; is not he whose brain grows bewildered with the meaning of some musical cadence which has never before arrested his attention.

Amid frequent and thoughtful endeavors to remember, amid earnest struggles to regather some token of the state of seeming nothingness into which my soul had lapsed, there have been moments when I have dreamed of success; there have been brief, very brief, periods when I have conjured up remembrances which the lucid reason of a later epoch assures me could have had reference only to that condition of seeming unconsciousness. These shadows of memory tell indistinctly of tall figures that lifted and bore me in silence down—down—still down—till a hideous dizziness oppressed me at the mere idea of the interminableness of the descent. They tell also of a vague horror at my heart, on account of that heart's unnatural stillness. Then comes a sense of sudden motionlessness throughout all things, as if those who bore me (a ghastly train!) had outrun, in the descent, the limits of the limitless and paused from the wearisomeness of their toil. After this I call to mind flatness and dampness, and then all is *madness*—the madness of a memory which busies itself among forbidden things.

Very suddenly there came back to my soul motion and sound—the tumultuous motion of the heart and, in my ears, the sound of its beating. Then a pause, in which all is blank. Then again sound and motion and touch, a tingling sensation pervading my frame. Then the mere consciousness of existence, without thought, a condition which lasted long. Then, very suddenly, *thought* and shuddering terror and earnest endeavor to comprehend my true state. Then a strong desire to lapse into insensibility. Then a rushing revival of soul and a successful effort to move. And now a full memory of the trial, of the judges, of the sable draperies, of the sentence, of the sickness, of the swoon. Then entire forgetfulness of all that followed, of all that a later day and much earnestness of endeavor have enabled me vaguely to recall.

So far, I had not opened my eyes. I felt that I lay upon my back, unbound. I reached out my hand, and it fell heavily upon something damp and hard. There I suffered it to remain for many minutes while I strove to imagine where and *what* I could be. I longed, yet dared not, to employ my vision. I dreaded the first glance at objects around me. It was not that I feared to look upon things horrible, but that I grew aghast, lest there should be *nothing* to see. At length, with a wild desperation at heart, I quickly unclosed my eyes. My worst thoughts, then, were confirmed. The blackness of eternal night encompassed me. I struggled for breath. The intensity of the darkness seemed to oppress and stifle me. The atmosphere was intolerably close. I still lay quietly and made effort to exercise my reason. I brought to mind the inquisitorial proceedings and attempted from that point to deduce my real condition. The sentence had passed, and it appeared to me that a very long interval of time had since elapsed. Yet not for a moment did I suppose myself actually dead. Such a supposition, notwithstanding what we read in fiction, is altogether inconsistent with real existence. But where and in what state was I? The condemned to death, I knew, perished usually at the autos-da-fé, and one of these had been held on the very night of the day of my trial. Had I been remanded to my dungeon to await the next sacrifice, which would not take place for many months? This, I at once saw, could not be. Victims had been in immediate demand. Moreover, my dungeon, as well as all the condemned cells at Toledo, had stone floors, and light was not altogether excluded.

A fearful idea now suddenly drove the blood in torrents upon my heart, and for a brief period I once more relapsed into insensibility. Upon recovering, I at once started to my feet, trembling convulsively in every fiber. I thrust my arms wildly above and around me in all directions. I felt nothing, yet dreaded to move a step, lest I should be impeded by the walls of a *tomb*. Perspiration burst from every pore and stood in cold big beads upon my forehead. The agony of suspense grew at length intolerable, and I cautiously moved forward, with my arms extended and my eyes straining from their sockets in the hope of catching some faint ray of light. I proceeded for many paces, but still all was blackness and vacancy. I breathed more freely. It seemed evident that mine was not, at least, the most hideous of fates.

And now, as I still continued to step cautiously onward, there came thronging upon my recollection a thousand vague rumors of the horrors of Toledo. Of the dungeons, there had been strange things narrated—fables, I had always deemed them, but yet strange and too ghastly to repeat, save in a whisper. Was I left to perish of starvation in this subterranean world of darkness? Or what fate, perhaps even more fearful, awaited me? That the result would be death, and a death of more than customary bitterness, I knew too well the character of my judges to doubt. The mode and the hour were all that occupied or distracted me.

My outstretched hands at length encountered some

solid obstruction. It was a wall, seemingly of stone masonry—very smooth, slimy, and cold. I followed it up, stepping with all the careful distrust with which certain antique narratives had inspired me. This process, however, afforded me no means of ascertaining the dimensions of my dungeon, as I might make its circuit and return to the point whence I set out without being aware of the fact, so perfectly uniform seemed the wall. I therefore sought the knife which had been in my pocket when I had been led into the inquisitorial chamber, but it was gone; my clothes had been exchanged for a wrapper of coarse serge. I had thought of forcing the blade in some minute crevice of the masonry, so as to identify my point of departure. The difficulty, nevertheless, was but trivial, although, in the disorder of my fancy, it seemed at first insuperable. I tore a part of the hem from the robe and placed the fragment at full length and at right angles to the wall. In groping my way around the prison, I could not fail to encounter this rag, upon completing the circuit. So, at least, I thought, but I had not counted upon the extent of the dungeon or upon my own weakness. The ground was moist and slippery. I staggered onward for some time, when I stumbled and fell. My excessive fatigue induced me to remain prostrate, and sleep soon overtook me as I lay.

Upon awaking and stretching forth an arm, I found beside me a loaf and a pitcher of water. I was too much exhausted to reflect upon this circumstance but ate and drank with avidity. Shortly afterward I resumed my tour around the prison and, with much toil, came at last upon the fragment of the serge. Up to the period when I fell, I had counted fifty-two paces, and, upon resuming my walk, I had counted forty-eight more, when I arrived at the rag. There were in all, then, a hundred paces; and, admitting two paces to the yard, I presumed the dungeon to be fifty yards in circuit. I had met, however, with many angles in the wall, and thus I could form no guess at the shape of the vault, for vault I could not help supposing it to be.

I had little object—certainly no hope—in these researches, but a vague curiosity prompted me to continue them. Quitting the wall, I resolved to cross the area of the enclosure. At first I proceeded with extreme caution, for the floor, although seemingly of solid material, was treacherous with slime. At length, however, I took courage and did not hesitate to step firmly, endeavoring to cross in as direct a line as possible. I had advanced some ten or twelve paces in this manner, when the remnant of the torn hem of my robe became entangled between my legs. I stepped on it and fell violently on my face.

In the confusion attending my fall, I did not immediately apprehend a somewhat startling circumstance, which yet, a few seconds afterward, while I still lay prostrate, arrested my attention. It was this: My chin rested upon the floor of the prison, but my lips and the upper portion of the head, although seemingly at less elevation than the chin, touched nothing. At the same time, my forehead seemed bathed in a clammy vapor, and the peculiar smell of decayed fungus arose to my nostrils. I put forward my arm and shuddered to find that I had fallen at the very brink of a circular pit, whose extent, of course, I had no means of ascertaining at the moment. Groping about the masonry just below the margin, I succeeded in dislodging a small fragment and let it fall into the abyss. For many seconds I hearkened to its reverberations as it dashed against the sides of the chasm in its descent; at length there was a sullen plunge into water, succeeded by loud echoes. At the same moment there came a sound resembling the quick opening and as rapid closing of a door overhead, while a faint gleam of light flashed suddenly through the gloom and as suddenly faded away.

I saw clearly the doom which had been prepared for me and congratulated myself upon the timely accident by which I had escaped. Another step before my fall and the world had seen me no more, and the death just avoided was of that very character which I had regarded as fabulous and frivolous in the tales respecting the Inquisition. To the victims of its tyranny, there was the choice of death with its direst physical agonies or death with its most hideous moral horrors. I had been reserved for the latter. By long suffering, my nerves had been unstrung, until I trembled at the sound of my own voice and had become in every respect a fitting subject for the species of torture which awaited me.

Shaking in every limb, I groped my way back to the wall—resolving there to perish, rather than risk the terrors of the wells, of which my imagination now pictured many in various positions about the dungeon. In other conditions of mind, I might have had courage to end my misery at once by a plunge into one of these abysses, but now I was the veriest of cowards. Neither could I forget what I had read of these pits—that the *sudden* extinction of life formed no part of their most horrible plan.

Agitation of spirit kept me awake for many long hours, but at length I again slumbered. Upon arousing, I found by my side, as before, a loaf and a pitcher of water. A burning thirst consumed me, and I emptied the vessel at a draft. It must have been drugged, for scarcely had I drunk before I became irresistibly drowsy. A deep sleep fell upon me—a sleep like that of death. How long it lasted, of course, I know not; but when once again I unclosed my eyes, the objects around me were visible. By a wild, sulfurous luster, the origin of which I could not at first determine, I was enabled to see the extent and aspect of the prison.

In its size, I had been greatly mistaken. The whole circuit of its walls did not exceed twenty-five yards. For some minutes this fact occasioned in me a world of vain trouble—vain, indeed, for what could be of less importance, under the terrible circumstances which environed me, than the mere dimensions of my dungeon? But my soul took a wild interest in trifles, and I busied myself in endeavors to account for the error I had committed in my measurement. The truth at length flashed upon me. In my first attempt at exploration, I had counted fifty-two paces up to the period when I fell; I must then have been within a pace or two of the fragment of serge; in fact, I had nearly performed the circuit of the vault. I then slept, and, upon awaking, I must have returned upon my steps, thus supposing the circuit nearly double what it actually was. My confusion of mind prevented me from observing that I began my tour with the wall to the left and ended it with the wall to the right.

I had been deceived, too, in respect to the shape of the enclosure. In feeling my way, I had found many angles and thus deduced an idea of great irregularity, so potent is the effect of total darkness upon one arousing from lethargy or sleep! The angles were simply those of a few slight depressions or niches at odd intervals. The general shape of the prison was square. What I had taken for masonry seemed now to be iron or some other metal in huge plates, whose sutures or joints occasioned the depression. The entire surface of this metallic enclosure was rudely daubed in all the hideous and repulsive devices to which the charnel superstition of the monks had given rise. The figures of fiends, in aspects of menace, with skeleton forms and other more really fearful images, overspread and disfigured the walls. I observed that the outlines of these monstrosities were sufficiently distinct, but that the colors seemed faded and blurred, as if from the effects of a damp atmosphere. I now noticed the floor, too, which was of stone. In the center yawned the circular pit from whose jaws I had escaped, but it was the only one in the dungeon.

All this I saw indistinctly and by much effort, for my personal condition had been greatly changed during slumber. I now lay upon my back and at full length on a species of low framework of wood. To this I was securely bound by a long strap resembling a surcingle. It passed in many convolutions about my limbs and body, leaving at liberty only my head and my left arm, to such extent that I could, by dint of much exertion, supply myself with food from an earthen dish which lay by my side on the floor. I saw, to my horror, that the pitcher had been removed. I say to my horror, for I was consumed with intolerable thirst. This thirst it appeared to be the design of my persecutors to stimulate, for the food in the dish was meat, pungently seasoned.

Looking upward, I surveyed the ceiling of my prison. It was some thirty or forty feet overhead and constructed much as the side walls. In one of its panels, a very singular figure riveted my whole attention. It was the painted figure of Time as he is commonly represented, save that, in lieu of a scythe, he held what at a casual glance I supposed to be the pictured image of a huge pendulum, such as we see on antique clocks. There was something, however, in the appearance of this machine which caused me to regard it more attentively. While I gazed directly upward at it (for its position was immediately over my own), I fancied that I saw it in motion. In an instant afterward, the fancy was confirmed. Its sweep was brief and, of course, slow. I watched it for some minutes, somewhat in fear but more in wonder. Wearied at length with observing its dull movement, I turned my eyes upon the other objects in the cell.

A slight noise attracted my notice, and, looking to the floor, I saw several enormous rats traversing it. They had issued from the well, which lay just within view to my right. Even then, while I gazed, they came up in troops hurriedly, with ravenous eyes, allured by the scent of the meat. From this, it required much effort and attention to scare them away.

It might have been half an hour, perhaps even an hour (for I could take but imperfect note of time), before I again cast my eyes upward. What I then saw confounded and amazed me. The sweep of the pendulum had increased in extent by nearly a yard. As a natural consequence, its velocity was also much greater. But what mainly disturbed me was the idea that it had perceptibly *descended.* I now observed—with what horror, it is needless to say—that its nether extremity was formed of a crescent of glittering steel about a foot in length from horn to horn, the horns upward and the under edge evidently as keen as that of a razor. Like a razor, also, it seemed massy and heavy, tapering from the edge into a solid and broad structure above. It was appended to a weighty rod of brass, and the whole *hissed* as it swung through the air.

I could no longer doubt the doom prepared for me by monkish ingenuity in torture. My cognizance of the pit had become known to the inquisitorial agents—*the pit,* whose horrors had been destined for so bold a recusant as myself; *the pit,* typical of hell and regarded by rumor as the Ultima Thule of all their punishments. The plunge into this pit I had avoided by the merest of accidents,

and I knew that surprise or entrapment into torment formed an important portion of all the grotesquerie of these dungeon deaths. Since I had not fallen, it was no part of the demon plan to hurl me into the abyss, and thus (there being no alternative) a different and a milder destruction awaited me. Milder! I half smiled in my agony as I thought of such application of such a term.

What boots it to tell of the long, long hours of horror more than mortal, during which I counted the rushing oscillations of the steel! Inch by inch—line by line—with a descent only appreciable at intervals that seemed ages—down and still down it came! Days passed—it might have been that many days passed—ere it swept so closely over me as to fan me with its acrid breath. The odor of the sharp steel forced itself into my nostrils. I prayed—I wearied heaven with my prayer for its more speedy descent. I grew frantically mad and struggled to force myself upward against the sweep of the fearful scimitar. And then I fell suddenly calm and lay smiling at the glittering death, as a child at some rare bauble.

There was another interval of utter insensibility; it was brief, for, upon again lapsing into life, I noted that there had been no perceptible descent in the pendulum. But it might have been long—for I knew there were demons who took note of my swoon and who could have arrested the vibration at pleasure. Upon my recovery, too, I felt very—oh! inexpressibly—sick and weak, as if through long inanition. Even amid the agonies of that period, the human nature craved food. With painful effort, I outstretched my left arm as far as my bonds permitted and took possession of the small remnant which had been spared me by the rats. As I put a portion of it within my lips, there rushed to my mind a half-formed thought of joy—of hope. Yet what business had *I* with hope? It was, as I say, a half-formed thought—man has many such, which are never completed. I felt that it was of joy—of hope—but I felt also that it had perished in its formation. In vain I struggled to perfect—to regain it. Long suffering had nearly annihilated all my ordinary powers of mind. I was an imbecile—an idiot.

The vibration of the pendulum was at right angles to my length. I saw that the crescent was designed to cross the region of the heart. It would fray the serge of my robe; it would return and repeat its operation—again—and again. Notwithstanding its terrifically wide sweep (some thirty feet or more) and the hissing vigor of its descent, sufficient to sunder these very walls of iron, still, the fraying of my robe would be all that, for several minutes, it would accomplish; and at this thought I paused. I dared not go further than this reflection. I dwelt upon it with a pertinacity of attention—as if, in so dwelling, I could arrest *here* the descent of the steel. I forced myself to ponder upon the sound of the crescent as it should pass across the garment—upon the peculiar thrilling sensation which the friction of cloth produces on the nerves. I pondered upon all this frivolity until my teeth were on edge.

Down—steadily down it crept. I took a frenzied pleasure in contrasting its downward with its lateral velocity. To the right—to the left—far and wide—with the shriek of a damned spirit! To my heart, with the stealthy pace of the tiger! I alternately laughed and howled as the one or the other idea grew predominant.

Down—certainly, relentlessly down! It vibrated within three inches of my bosom! I struggled violently—furiously—to free my left arm. This was free only from the elbow to the hand. I could reach the latter, from the platter beside me to my mouth, with great effort, but no farther. Could I have broken the fastenings above the elbow, I would have seized and attempted to arrest the pendulum. I might as well have attempted to arrest an avalanche!

Down—still unceasingly—still inevitably down! I gasped and struggled at each vibration. I shrunk convulsively at its every sweep. My eyes followed its outward or upward whirls with the eagerness of the most unmeaning despair; they closed themselves spasmodically at the descent, although death would have been a relief. Oh, how unspeakable! I quivered in every nerve to think how slight a sinking of the machinery would precipitate that keen, glistening ax upon my bosom. It was *hope* that prompted the nerve to quiver, the frame to shrink. It was *hope*—the hope that triumphs on the rack—that whispers to the death-condemned even in the dungeons of the Inquisition.

I saw that some ten or twelve vibrations would bring the steel in actual contact with my robe, and with this observation there suddenly came over my spirit all the keen, collected calmness of despair. For the first time during many hours, or perhaps days, I *thought*. It now occurred to me that the bandage or surcingle which enveloped me was *unique*. I was tied by no separate cord. The first stroke of the razor-like crescent athwart any portion of the band would so detach it that it might be unwound from my person by means of my left hand. But how fearful, in that case, the proximity of the steel! The result of the slightest struggle, how deadly! Was it likely, moreover, that the minions of the torturer had not foreseen and provided for this possibility? Was it probable that the bandage crossed my bosom in the track of the pendulum? Dreading to find my faint and, as it seemed, my last hope frustrated, I so far elevated my head as to obtain a distinct view of my breast. The surcingle enveloped my limbs and body close in all directions *save in the very path of the destroying crescent.*

Scarcely had I dropped my head back into its original position when there flashed upon my mind what I cannot better describe than as the unformed half of that idea of deliverance to which I have previously alluded, of which a moiety only floated indeterminately through my brain when I raised food to my burning lips. The whole thought was now present—feeble, scarcely sane, scarcely definite, but still entire. I proceeded at once, with the nervous energy of despair, to attempt its execution.

For many hours the immediate vicinity of the low framework upon which I lay had been literally swarming with rats. They were wild, bold, ravenous, their red eyes glaring upon me as if they waited but for motionlessness on my part to make me their prey. *To what food,* I thought, *have they been accustomed in the well?*

They had devoured, in spite of all my efforts to prevent them, all but a small remnant of the contents of the dish. I had fallen into an habitual seesaw or wave of my hand about the platter, and at length the unconscious uniformity of the movement deprived it of effect. In their voracity, the vermin frequently fastened their sharp fangs in my fingers. With the particles of the oily and spicy viand which now remained, I thoroughly rubbed the bandage wherever I could reach it; then, raising my hand from the floor, I lay breathlessly still.

At first the ravenous animals were startled and terrified at the change—at the cessation of movement. They shrank alarmedly back; many sought the well. But this was only for a moment. I had not counted in vain upon their voracity. Observing that I remained without motion, one or two of the boldest leaped upon the framework and smelled at the surcingle. This seemed the signal for a general rush. Forth from the well they hurried in fresh troops. They clung to the wood; they overran it and leaped in hundreds upon my person. The measured movement of the pendulum disturbed them not at all. Avoiding its strokes, they busied themselves with the anointed bandage. They pressed, they swarmed upon me in ever accumulating heaps. They writhed upon my throat; their cold lips sought my own; I was half stifled by their thronging pressure; disgust for which the world has no name swelled my bosom and chilled with heavy clamminess my heart. Yet one minute, and I felt that the struggle would be over. Plainly I perceived the loosening of the bandage. I knew that in more than one place it must be already severed. With a more than human resolution I lay *still.*

Nor had I erred in my calculations, nor had I endured in vain. I at length felt that I was *free*. The surcingle hung in ribbons from my body. But the stroke of the pendulum already pressed upon my bosom. It had divided the serge of the robe. It had cut through the linen beneath. Twice again it swung, and a sharp sense of pain shot through every nerve. But the moment of escape had arrived. At a wave of my hand, my deliverers hurried tumultuously away. With a steady movement—cautious, sidelong, shrinking, and slow—I slid from the embrace of the bandage and beyond the reach of the scimitar. For the moment, at least, *I was free*.

Free! And in the grasp of the Inquisition! I had scarcely stepped from my wooden bed of horror upon the stone floor of the prison, when the motion of the hellish machine ceased, and I beheld it drawn up by some invisible force through the ceiling. This was a lesson which I took desperately to heart. My every motion was undoubtedly watched. Free! I had but escaped death in one form of agony to be delivered unto worse than death in some other. With that thought, I rolled my eyes nervously around on the barriers of iron that hemmed me in. Something unusual—some change, which at first I could not appreciate distinctly—it was obvious, had taken place in the apartment. For many minutes of a dreamy and trembling abstraction, I busied myself in vain, unconnected conjecture. During this period I became aware, for the first time, of the origin of the sulfurous light which illumined the cell. It proceeded from a fissure about half an inch in width extending entirely around the prison at the base of the walls, which thus appeared, and were, completely separated from the floor. I endeavored, but, of course, in vain, to look through the aperture.

As I arose from the attempt, the mystery of the alteration in the chamber broke at once upon my understanding. I have observed that, although the outlines of the figures upon the walls were sufficiently distinct, yet the colors seemed blurred and indefinite. These colors had now assumed and were momentarily assuming a startling and most intense brilliancy that gave to the spectral and fiendish portraitures an aspect that might have thrilled even firmer nerves than my own. Demon eyes, of a wild and ghastly vivacity, glared upon me from a thousand directions, where none had been visible before, and gleamed with the lurid luster of a fire that I could not force my imagination to regard as unreal.

Unreal! Even while I breathed, there came to my nostrils the breath of the vapor of heated iron! A suffocating odor pervaded the prison! A deeper glow settled each moment in the eyes that glared at my agonies! A richer tint of crimson diffused itself over the pictured horrors of blood. I panted! I gasped for breath! There could be no doubt of the design of my tormentors—oh, most unrelenting! Oh, most demoniac of men! I shrank from the glowing metal to the center of the cell. Amid the thought of the fiery destruction that impended, the idea of the coolness of the well came over my soul like balm. I rushed to its deadly brink. I threw my straining vision below. The glare from the enkindled roof illumined its inmost recesses. Yet, for a wild moment, did my spirit refuse to comprehend the meaning of what I saw. At length it forced—it wrestled—its way into my soul; it burned itself in upon my shuddering reason. Oh, for a voice to speak! Oh, horror! Oh, any horror but this! With a shriek, I rushed from the margin and buried my face in my hands, weeping bitterly.

The heat rapidly increased, and once again I looked up, shuddering, as if with a fit of the ague. There had been a second change in the cell—and now the change was obviously in the *form*. As before, it was in vain that I at first endeavored to appreciate or understand what was taking place. But not long was I left in doubt. The inquisitorial vengeance had been hurried by my twofold escape, and there was to be no more dallying with the King of Terrors. The room had been square. I saw that two of its iron angles were now acute—two, consequently, obtuse. The fearful difference quickly increased, with a low rumbling, or moaning, sound. In an instant the apartment had shifted its form into that of a lozenge. But the alteration stopped not here—I neither hoped nor desired it to stop. I could have clasped the red walls to my bosom as a garment of eternal peace. "Death," I said, "any death but that of the pit!" Fool! Might I not have known that *into the pit* it was the object of the burning iron to urge me? Could I resist its glow? Or, if even that, could I withstand its pressure? And now, flatter and flatter grew the lozenge, with a rapidity that left me no time for contemplation. Its center, and, of course, its greatest width, came just over the yawning gulf. I shrank back—but the closing walls pressed me resistlessly onward. At length, for my seared and writhing body, there was no longer an inch of foothold on the firm floor of the prison. I struggled no more, but the agony of my soul found vent in one loud, long, and final scream of despair. I felt that I tottered upon the brink—I averted my eyes—

There was a discordant hum of human voices! There was a loud blast, as of many trumpets! There was a harsh grating, as of a thousand thunders! The fiery walls rushed back! An outstretched arm caught my own as I fell, fainting, into the abyss. It was that of General Lasalle. The French army had entered Toledo. The Inquisition was in the hands of its enemies.

The Facts in the Case of M. Valdemar

OF COURSE I shall not pretend to consider it any matter for wonder that the extraordinary case of M. Valdemar has excited discussion. It would have been a miracle had it not—especially under the circumstances. Through the desire of all parties concerned to keep the affair from the public, at least for the present, or until we had further opportunities for investigation—through our endeavors to effect this—a garbled or exaggerated account made its way into society and became the source of many unpleasant misrepresentations and, very naturally, of a great deal of disbelief.

It is now rendered necessary that I give the *facts*—as far as I comprehend them myself. They are, succinctly, these:

My attention for the last three years had been repeatedly drawn to the subject of mesmerism, and about nine months ago it occurred to me, quite suddenly, that in the series of experiments made hitherto there had been a very remarkable and most unaccountable omission: No person had as yet been mesmerized *in articulo mortis.** It remained to be seen, first, whether in such condition there existed in the patient any susceptibility to the magnetic influence; second, whether, if any existed, it was

*"in the jaws of death"

impaired or increased by the condition; third, to what extent or for how long a period the encroachments of death might be arrested by the process. There were other points to be ascertained, but these most excited my curiosity—the last in especial, from the immensely important character of its consequences.

In looking around me for some subject by whose means I might test these particulars, I was brought to think of my friend, M. Ernest Valdemar, the well-known compiler of the *Bibliotheca Forensica* and author (under the nom de plume of Issachar Marx) of the Polish versions of *Wallenstein* and *Gargantua*. M. Valdemar, who has resided principally at Harlem, New York, since the year 1839, is (or was) particularly noticeable for the extreme spareness of his person—his lower limbs much resembling those of John Randolph—and also for the whiteness of his whiskers, in violent contrast to the blackness of his hair—the latter, in consequence, being generally mistaken for a wig. His temperament was markedly nervous and rendered him a good subject for mesmeric experiment. On two or three occasions, I had put him to sleep with little difficulty but was disappointed in other results which his peculiar constitution had naturally led me to expect. His will was at no period positively or thoroughly under my control, and, in regard to clairvoyance, I could accomplish with him nothing to be relied upon. I always attributed my failure at these points to the disordered state of his health. For some months previous to my becoming acquainted with him, his physicians had declared him in a confirmed phthisis. It was his custom, indeed, to speak calmly of his approaching dissolution as of a matter neither to be avoided nor regretted.

When the ideas to which I have alluded first occurred to me, it was, of course, very natural that I should think of M. Valdemar. I knew the steady philosophy of the man too well to apprehend any scruples from *him,* and he had no relatives in America who would be likely to interfere. I spoke to him frankly on the subject, and, to my surprise, his interest seemed vividly excited. I say to my surprise, for, although he had always yielded his person freely to my experiments, he had never before given me any tokens of sympathy with what I did. His disease was of that character which would admit of exact calculation in respect to the epoch of its termination in death, and it was finally arranged between us that he would send for me about twenty-four hours before the period announced by his physicians as that of his decease.

It is now rather more than seven months since I received from M. Valdemar himself the subjoined note:

> My Dear P——,
>
> You may as well come *now*. D—— and F—— are agreed that I cannot hold out beyond tomorrow midnight, and I think they have hit the time very nearly.
>
> Valdemar

I received this note within half an hour after it was written, and in fifteen minutes more I was in the dying man's chamber. I had not seen him for ten days and was appalled by the fearful alteration which the brief interval had wrought in him. His face wore a leaden hue, the eyes were utterly lusterless, and the emaciation was so extreme that the skin had been broken through by the cheekbones. His expectoration was excessive. The pulse was barely perceptible. He retained, nevertheless, in a very remarkable manner, both his mental power and a certain degree of physical strength. He spoke with distinctness, took some palliative medicines without aid, and, when I entered the room, was occupied in penciling memoranda in a pocketbook. He was propped up in bed by pillows. Drs. D—— and F—— were in attendance.

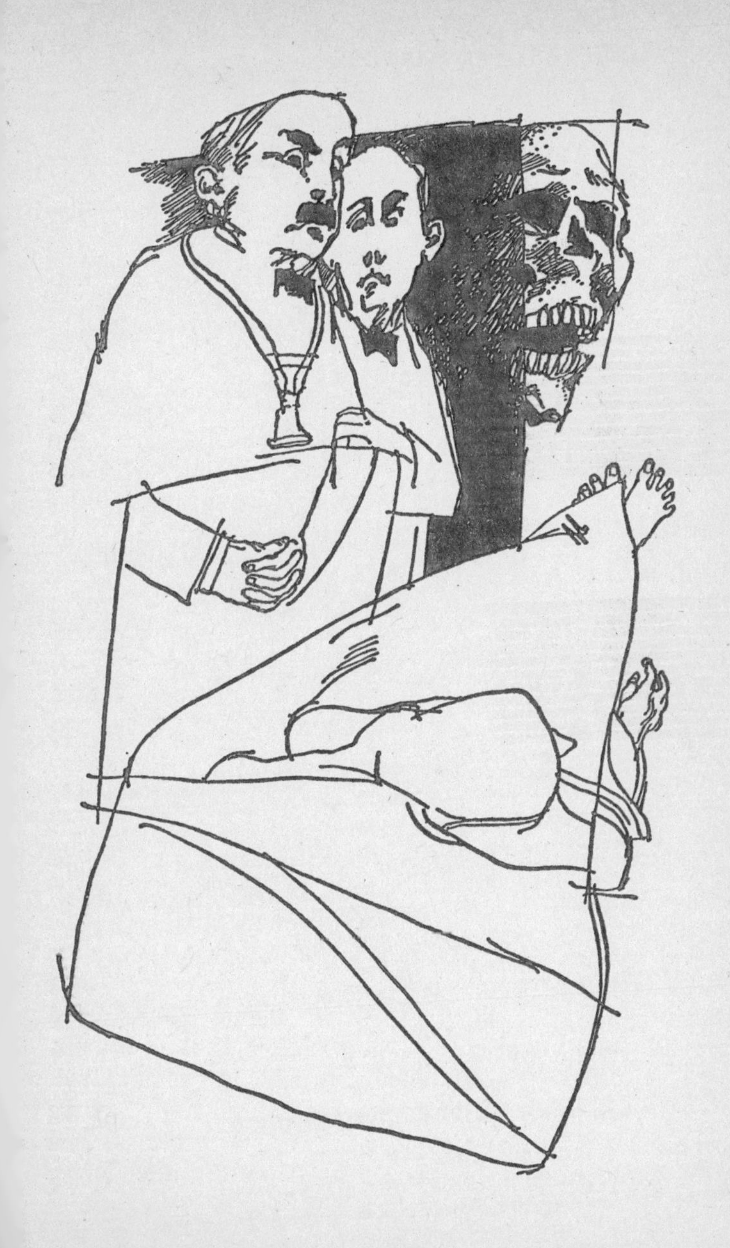

After pressing Valdemar's hand, I took these gentlemen aside and obtained from them a minute account of the patient's condition. The left lung had been for eighteen months in a semiosseous or cartilaginous state and was, of course, entirely useless for all purposes of vitality. The right, in its upper portion, was also partially if not thoroughly ossified, while the lower region was merely a mass of purulent tubercles running one into another. Several extensive perforations existed, and at one point permanent adhesion to the ribs had taken place. These appearances in the right lobe were of comparatively recent date. The ossification had proceeded with very unusual rapidity; no sign of it had been discovered a month before, and the adhesion had been observed only during the three previous days. In addition to the phthisis, the patient was suspected of aneurism of the aorta, but on this point the osseous symptoms rendered an exact diagnosis impossible. It was the opinion of both physicians that M. Valdemar would die about midnight on the morrow (Sunday). It was then seven o'clock on Saturday evening.

On quitting the invalid's bedside to hold conversation with me, Drs. D—— and F—— had bidden him a final farewell. It had not been their intention to return, but, at my request, they agreed to look in upon the patient about ten the next night.

When they had gone, I spoke freely with M. Valdemar on the subject of his approaching dissolution as well as, more particularly, of the experiment proposed. He still professed himself quite willing and even anxious to have it made and urged me to commence it at once. A male and a female nurse were in attendance, but I did not feel myself altogether at liberty to engage in a task of this nature with no more reliable witnesses than these people, in case of sudden accident, might prove. I therefore postponed operations until about eight the next night, when the arrival of a medical student with whom I had some acquaintance (Mr. Theodore L——l) relieved me from further embarrassment. It had been my design, originally, to wait for the physicians; but I was induced to proceed, first, by the urgent entreaties of M. Valdemar, and second, by my conviction that I had not a moment to lose, as he was evidently sinking fast.

Mr. L——l was so kind as to accede to my desire that he would take notes of all that occurred, and it is from his memoranda that what I now have to relate is, for the most part, either condensed or copied verbatim.

It wanted about five minutes of eight when, taking the patient's hand, I begged him to state as distinctly as he could to Mr. L——l whether he (M. Valdemar) was entirely willing that I should make the experiment of mesmerizing him in his then condition.

He replied feebly, yet quite audibly, "Yes, I wish to be mesmerized," adding immediately afterward, "I fear you have deferred it too long."

While he spoke thus, I commenced the passes which I had already found most effectual in subduing him. He was evidently influenced with the first lateral stroke of my hand across his forehead, but, although I exerted all my powers, no further perceptible effect was induced until some minutes after ten o'clock, when Drs. D—— and F—— called, according to appointment. I explained to them in a few words what I designed, and, as they posed no objection, saying that the patient was already in the death agony, I proceeded without hesitation—exchanging, however, the lateral passes for downward ones and directing my gaze entirely into the right eye of the sufferer.

By this time his pulse was imperceptible, and his breathing was stertorous and at intervals of half a minute.

This condition was nearly unaltered for a quarter of an hour. At the expiration of this period, however, a natural, although a very deep, sigh escaped the bosom of the dying man, and the stertorous breathing ceased—that is to say, its stertorousness was no longer apparent; the intervals were undiminished. The patient's extremities were of an icy coldness.

At five minutes before eleven I perceived unequivocal signs of the mesmeric influence. The glassy roll of the eye was changed for that expression of uneasy *inward* examination which is never seen except in cases of sleep-waking and which is quite impossible to mistake. With a few rapid lateral passes, I made the lids quiver, as in incipient sleep, and with a few more I closed them altogether. I was not satisfied, however, with this but continued the manipulations vigorously and with the fullest exertion of the will, until I had completely stiffened the limbs of the slumberer, after placing them in a seemingly easy position. The legs were at full length; the arms were nearly so and reposed on the bed at a moderate distance from the loins. The head was very slightly elevated.

When I had accomplished this, it was fully midnight, and I requested the gentlemen present to examine M. Valdemar's condition. After a few experiments, they admitted him to be in an unusually perfect state of mesmeric trance. The curiosity of both the physicians was greatly excited. Dr. D—— resolved at once to remain with the patient all night, while Dr. F—— took leave, with a promise to return at daybreak. Mr. L——l and the nurses remained.

We left M. Valdemar entirely undisturbed until about three o'clock in the morning, when I approached him and found him in precisely the same condition as when Dr. F—— went away—that is to say, he lay in the same position; the pulse was imperceptible; the breathing was gentle (scarcely noticeable, unless through the application of a mirror to the lips); the eyes were closed naturally; and the limbs were as rigid and as cold as marble. Still, the general appearance was certainly not that of death.

As I approached M. Valdemar, I made a kind of half effort to influence his right arm into pursuit of my own as I passed the latter gently to and fro above his person. In such experiments with this patient, I had never perfectly succeeded before, and assuredly I had little thought of succeeding now; but, to my astonishment, his arm very readily, although feebly, followed every direction I assigned it with mine. I determined to hazard a few words of conversation.

"M. Valdemar," I said, "are you asleep?" He made no answer, but I perceived a tremor about the lips and was thus induced to repeat the question, again and again.

At this third repetition, his whole frame was agitated by a very slight shivering. The eyelids unclosed themselves so far as to display a white line of a ball, the lips moved sluggishly, and, from between them, in a barely audible whisper, issued the words: "Yes—asleep now. Do not wake me! Let me die so!"

I here felt the limbs and found them as rigid as ever. The right arm, as before, obeyed the direction of my hand. I questioned the sleep-waker again.

"Do you still feel pain in the breast, M. Valdemar?"

The answer now was immediate but even less audible than before: "No pain—I am dying."

I did not think it advisable to disturb him further just then, and nothing more was said or done until the arrival of Dr. F——, who came a little before sunrise and expressed unbounded astonishment at finding the patient still alive. After feeling the pulse and applying a mirror to the lips, he requested me to speak to the sleep-waker again.

I did so, saying, "M. Valdemar, do you still sleep?"

As before, some minutes elapsed ere a reply was made, and during the interval the dying man seemed to be collecting his energies to speak. At my fourth repetition of the question, he said very faintly, almost inaudibly, "Yes—still asleep—dying."

It was now the opinion, or rather the wish, of the physicians that M. Valdemar should be suffered to remain undisturbed in his present apparently tranquil condition until death should supervene; and this, it was generally agreed, must now take place within a few minutes. I concluded, however, to speak to him once more and merely repeated my previous question.

While I spoke, there came a marked change over the countenance of the sleep-waker. The eyes rolled themselves slowly open, the pupils disappearing upwardly; the skin generally assumed a cadaverous hue, resembling not so much parchment as white paper; and the circular hectic spots, which hitherto had been strongly defined in the center of each cheek, *went out* at once. I use this expression because the suddenness of their departure put me in mind of nothing so much as the extinguishment of a candle by a puff of the breath. The upper lip, at the same time, writhed itself away from the teeth, which it had previously covered completely, while the lower jaw fell, with an audible jerk, leaving the mouth widely extended and disclosing in full view the swollen and blackened tongue. I presume that no member of the party then present had been unaccustomed to deathbed horrors, but so hideous beyond conception was the appearance of M. Valdemar at this moment that there was a general shrinking back from the region of the bed.

I now feel that I have reached a point of this narrative at which every reader will be startled into positive disbelief. It is my business, however, simply to proceed.

There was no longer the faintest sign of vitality in M. Valdemar, and, concluding him to be dead, we were consigning him to the charge of the nurses, when a strong vibratory motion was observable in the tongue. This continued for perhaps a minute. At the expiration of this period, there issued from the distended and motionless jaws a voice—such as it would be madness in me to attempt describing. There are, indeed, two or three epithets which might be considered as applicable to it in part; I might say, for example, that the sound was harsh and broken and hollow, but the hideous whole is indescribable, for the simple reason that no similar sounds have ever jarred upon the ear of humanity. There were two particulars, nevertheless, which I thought then, and still think, might fairly be stated as characteristic of the intonation—as well adapted to convey some idea of its unearthly peculiarity. In the first place, the voice seemed to reach our ears—at least mine—from a vast distance or from some deep cavern within the earth. In the second place, it impressed me (I fear, indeed, that it will be impossible to make myself comprehended) as gelatinous or glutinous matters impress the sense of touch.

I have spoken both of "sound" and of "voice." I mean to say that the sound was one of distinct—of even wonderfully, thrillingly distinct—syllabification. M. Valdemar *spoke*—obviously in reply to the question I had propounded to him a few minutes before. I had asked him, it will be remembered, if he still slept. He now said,

"Yes—no—I *have been sleeping*—and now—now—*I am dead.*"

No person present even affected to deny or attempted to repress the unutterable, shuddering horror which these few words, thus uttered, were so well calculated to convey. Mr. L——l (the student) swooned. The nurses immediately left the chamber and could not be induced to return. My own impressions I would not pretend to render intelligible to the reader. For nearly an hour we busied ourselves silently—without the utterance of a word—in endeavors to revive Mr. L——l. When he came to himself, we addressed ourselves again to an investigation of M. Valdemar's condition.

It remained in all respects as I have last described it, with the exception that the mirror no longer afforded evidence of respiration. An attempt to draw blood from the arm failed. I should mention, too, that this limb was no further subject to my will. I endeavored in vain to make it follow the direction of my hand. The only real indication, indeed, of the mesmeric influence was now found in the vibratory movement of the tongue whenever I addressed M. Valdemar a question. He seemed to be making an effort to reply but had no longer sufficient volition. To queries put to him by any person other than me, he seemed utterly insensible—although I endeavored to place each member of the company in mesmeric rapport with him. I believe that I have now related all that is necessary to an understanding of the sleep-waker's state at this epoch. Other nurses were procured, and at ten o'clock I left the house in company with the two physicians and Mr. L——l.

In the afternoon we all called again to see the patient. His condition remained precisely the same. We had now some discussion as to the propriety and feasibility of awakening him, but we had little difficulty in agreeing that no good purpose would be served by so doing. It was evident that, so far, death (or what is usually termed death) had been arrested by the mesmeric process. It seemed clear to us all that to awaken M. Valdemar would be merely to insure his instant, or at least speedy, dissolution.

From this period until the close of last week—*an interval of nearly seven months*—we continued to make daily calls at M. Valdemar's house, accompanied now and then by medical and other friends. All this time the sleep-waker remained *exactly* as I have last described him. The nurses' attentions were continual.

It was on Friday last that we finally resolved to make the experiment of awakening, or attempting to awaken him, and it is the (perhaps) unfortunate result of this latter experiment which has given rise to so much discussion in private circles—to so much of what I cannot help thinking unwarranted popular feeling.

For the purpose of relieving M. Valdemar from the mesmeric trance, I made use of the customary passes. These, for a time, were unsuccessful. The first indication of revival was afforded by a partial descent of the iris. It was observed as especially remarkable that this lowering of the pupil was accompanied by the profuse outflowing of a yellowish ichor (from beneath the lids) of a pungent and highly offensive odor.

It was now suggested that I should attempt to influence the patient's arm, as heretofore. I made the attempt and failed.

Dr. F—— then intimated a desire to have me put a question. I did so, as follows: "M. Valdemar, can you explain to us what are your feelings or wishes now?"

There was an instant return of the hectic circles on the

cheeks; the tongue quivered, or rather rolled, violently in the mouth (although the jaws and lips remained rigid as before), and at length the same hideous voice which I have already described broke forth: "For God's sake! Quick—quick! Put me to sleep—or, quick!—waken me! Quick! *I say to you that I am dead!*"

I was thoroughly unnerved and for an instant remained undecided what to do. At first I made an endeavor to recompose the patient, but, failing in this through total abeyance of the will, I retraced my steps and as earnestly struggled to awaken him. In this attempt, I soon saw that I should be successful—or at least I soon fancied that my success would be complete—and I am sure that all in the room were prepared to see the patient awaken.

For what really occurred, however, it is quite impossible that any human being could have been prepared.

As I rapidly made the mesmeric passes, amid ejaculations of "Dead! Dead!" absolutely *bursting* from the tongue and not from the lips of the sufferer, his whole frame at once—within the space of a single minute or less—shrunk, crumbled, absolutely *rotted* away beneath my hands. Upon the bed, before that whole company, there lay a nearly liquid mass of loathsome—of detestable—putrescence.

Berenice

MISERY IS MANIFOLD. The wretchedness of earth is multiform. Overarching the wide horizon as the rainbow, its hues are as various as the hues of that arch, as distinct, too, yet as intimately blended. Overarching the wide horizon as the rainbow! How is it that from beauty I have derived a type of unloveliness? From the covenant of peace a simile of sorrow? But as in ethics evil is a consequence of good, so, in fact, out of joy is sorrow born. Either the memory of past bliss is the anguish of today, or the agonies which *are* have their origin in the ecstasies which *might have been.*

My baptismal name is Egoeus; that of my family I will not mention. Yet there are no towers in the land more time-honored than my gloomy, gray hereditary halls. Our line has been called a race of visionaries, and in many striking particulars—in the character of the family mansion, in the frescoes of the chief saloon, in the tapestries of the dormitories, in the chiseling of some buttresses in the armory, but more especially in the gallery of antique paintings, in the fashion of the library chamber, and lastly, in the very peculiar nature of the library's contents—there is more than sufficient evidence to warrant the belief.

The recollections of my earliest years are connected with that chamber and with its volumes, of which latter

I will say no more. Here died my mother. Herein was I born. But it is mere idleness to say that I had not lived before, that the soul has no previous existence. You deny it? Let us not argue the matter. Convinced myself, I seek not to convince. There is, however, a remembrance of aerial forms, of spiritual and meaning eyes, of sounds musical yet sad; a remembrance which will not be excluded, a memory like a shadow, vague, variable, indefinite, unsteady; and like a shadow, too, in the impossibility of my getting rid of it while the sunlight of my reason shall exist.

In that chamber was I born. Thus awaking from the long night of what seemed, but was not, nonentity, at once into the very regions of fairyland, into a palace of imagination, into the wild dominions of monastic thought and erudition, it is not singular that I gazed around me with a startled and ardent eye, that I loitered away my boyhood in books and dissipated my youth in reverie; but it *is* singular, as years rolled away and the noon of manhood found me in the mansion of my fathers, what stagnation there fell upon the springs of my life, wonderful how total an inversion took place in the character of my commonest thought. The realities of the world affected me as visions and as visions only, while the wild ideas of the land of dreams became, in turn, not the material of my everyday existence but in very deed that existence utterly and solely in itself.

Berenice and I were cousins, and we grew up together in my paternal halls. Yet differently we grew—I, ill of health and buried in gloom; she, agile, graceful, and overflowing with energy—hers the ramble on the hillside; mine the studies of the cloister. I, living within my own heart and addicted, body and soul, to the most intense and painful meditation; she, roaming carelessly through life, with no thought of the shadows in her path or the silent flight of the raven-winged hours. Berenice! I call upon her name—Berenice!—and from the gray ruins of memory, a thousand tumultuous recollections are startled at the sound! Ah, vividly is her image before me now, as in the early days of her lightheartedness and joy! O gorgeous yet fantastic beauty! O sylph amid the shrubberies of Arnheim! O Naiad among its fountains! And then, then all is mystery and terror and a tale which should not be told. Disease, a fatal disease, fell like the simoom upon her frame; and even while I gazed upon her, the spirit of change swept over her, pervading her mind, her habits, and her character, and in a manner the most subtle and terrible, disturbing even the identity of her person! Alas! The destroyer came and went! And the victim, where is she? I knew her not, or knew her no longer as Berenice!

Among the numerous train of maladies superinduced by that fatal and primary one which effected a revolution of so horrible a kind in the moral and physical being of my cousin may be mentioned, as the most distressing and obstinate in its nature, a species of epilepsy not unfrequently terminating in *trance* itself—trance very nearly resembling positive dissolution and from which her manner of recovery was, in most instances, startlingly abrupt. In the meantime my own disease—for I have been told that I should call it by no other appellation—my own disease, then, grew rapidly upon me and assumed finally a monomaniac character of a novel and extraordinary form—hourly and momently gaining vigor—and at length obtaining over me the most incomprehensible ascendancy. This monomania, if I must so term it, consisted in a morbid irritability of those properties of the mind called in metaphysical science the *attentive*. It is more than probable that I am not understood, but I fear, indeed, that it is in no manner possible to convey to the mind of the merely general reader an adequate idea of that nervous *intensity of interest* with which, in my case, the powers of meditation (not to speak technically) busied and buried themselves in the contemplation of even the most ordinary objects of the universe.

To muse for long, unwearied hours with my attention riveted to some frivolous device on the margin or in the typography of a book; to become absorbed, for the better part of a summer's day, in a quaint shadow falling aslant upon the tapestry or upon the floor; to lose myself, for an entire night, in watching the steady flame of a lamp or the embers of a fire; to dream away whole days over the perfume of a flower; to repeat monotonously some common word until the sound, by dint of frequent repetition, ceases to convey any idea whatever to the mind; to lose all sense of motion or physical existence, by means of absolute bodily quiescence, long and obstinately persevered in. Such were a few of the most common and least pernicious vagaries induced by a condition of the mental faculties—not, indeed, altogether unparalleled, but certainly bidding defiance to anything resembling analysis or explanation.

Yet let me not be misapprehended. The undue, earnest, and morbid attention thus excited by objects in their own nature frivolous must not be confounded in character with that ruminating propensity common to all mankind and more especially indulged in by persons of ardent imagination. It was not even, as might be at first supposed, an extreme condition or exaggeration of such propensity but primarily and essentially distinct and different. In the one instance, the dreamer or enthusiast, being interested by an object usually *not* frivolous, imperceptibly loses sight of this object in a wilderness of deductions and suggestions issuing therefrom, until, at the conclusion of a daydream *often replete with luxury,* he finds the *incitamentum,* or first cause, of his musings entirely vanished and forgotten. In my case, the primary object was *invariably frivolous,* although assuming, through the medium of my distempered vision, a refracted and unreal importance. Few deductions, if any, were made, and those few pertinaciously returned in upon the original object as a center. The meditations were *never* pleasurable, and, at the termination of the reverie, the first cause, so far from being out of sight, had attained that supernaturally exaggerated interest which was the prevailing feature of the disease. In a word, the powers of mind more particularly exercised were, with me, as I have said before, the *attentive* and are, with the daydreamer, the *speculative.*

My books, at this epoch, if they did not actually serve to irritate the disorder, partook, it will be perceived, largely in their imaginative and inconsequential nature, of the characteristic qualities of the disorder itself. I well remember, among others, the treatise of the noble Italian, Coelius Secundus Curio, *De Amplitudine Beati Regni Dei;* St. Augustine's great work, *The City of God;* and Tertullian's *De Carne Christi,* in which the periodical sentence, "*Mortuus est Dei filius; credible est quia ineptum est; et sepultus resurrexit; certum est quia impossible est,*"* occupied my undivided time for many weeks of laborious and fruitless investigation.

Thus it will appear that, shaken from its balance only by trivial things, my reason bore resemblance to that ocean crag spoken of by Ptolemy Hephaestion, which, steadily

*"The Son of God is dead; it is believable because it is unbelievable; and having been buried he has arisen; it is certain because it is impossible."

resisting the attacks of human violence and the fiercer fury of the waters and the winds, trembled only to the touch of the flower called asphodel. And although, to a careless thinker, it might appear a matter beyond doubt that the alteration produced by her unhappy malady in the *moral* condition of Berenice would afford me many objects for the exercise of that intense and abnormal meditation whose nature I have been at some trouble in explaining, yet such was not in any degree the case. In the lucid intervals of my infirmity, her calamity indeed gave me pain, and, taking deeply to heart that total wreck of her fair and gentle life, I did not fail to ponder frequently and bitterly upon the wonder-working means by which so strange a revolution had been so suddenly brought to pass. But these reflections partook not of the idiosyncrasy of my disease and were such as would have occurred under similar circumstances to the ordinary mass of mankind. True to its own character, my disorder reveled in the less important but more startling changes wrought in the *physical* frame of Berenice—in the singular and most appalling distortion of her personal identity.

During the brightest days of her unparalleled beauty, most surely I had never loved her. In the strange anomaly of my existence, feelings with me *had never been* of the heart, and my passions *always were* of the mind. Through the gray of the early morning—among the trellised shadows of the forest at noonday—and in the silence of my library at night—she had flitted by my eyes, and I had seen her—not as the living and breathing Berenice but as the Berenice of a dream; not as a being of the earth, earthly, but as the abstraction of such a being; not as a thing to admire but to analyze; not as an object of love but as the theme of the most abstruse, although desultory, speculation. And *now*—now I shuddered in her presence and grew pale at her approach. Yet, bitterly lamenting her fallen and desolate condition, I called to mind that she had loved me long, and, in an evil moment, I spoke to her of marriage.

And at length the period of our nuptials was approaching, when, upon an afternoon in the winter of the year—one of those unseasonably warm, calm, and misty days which are the nurse of the beautiful Halcyon—I sat (and sat, as I thought, alone) in the inner apartment of the library. But, uplifting my eyes, I saw that Berenice stood before me.

Was it my own excited imagination—or the misty influence of the atmosphere—or the uncertain twilight of the chamber—or the gray draperies which fell around her figure—that caused in it so vacillating and indistinct an outline? I could not tell. She spoke no word, and I—not for worlds could I have uttered a syllable. An icy chill ran through my frame; a sense of insufferable anxiety oppressed me; a consuming curiosity pervaded my soul; and, sinking back upon the chair, I remained for some time breathless and motionless, with my eyes riveted upon her person. Alas! Its emaciation was excessive, and not one vestige of the former being lurked in any single line of the contour. My burning glances at length fell upon the face.

The forehead was high and very pale and singularly placid, and the once jetty hair fell partially over it and overshadowed the hollow temples with innumerable ringlets, now of a vivid yellow and jarring discordantly, in their fantastic character, with the reigning melancholy of the countenance. The eyes were lifeless and lusterless and seemingly pupilless, and I shrank involuntarily from their glassy stare to the contemplation of the thin and shrunken lips. They parted, and in a smile of peculiar meaning, the *teeth* of the changed Berenice disclosed themselves slowly to my view. Would to God that I had never beheld them or that, having done so, I had died!

The shutting of a door disturbed me, and, looking up, I found that my cousin had departed from the chamber. But from the disordered chamber of my brain had not, alas! departed, and would not be driven away, the white and ghastly *spectrum* of the teeth. Not a speck on their surface—not a shade on their enamel—not an indenture in their edges—but what that brief period of her smile had sufficed to brand it upon my memory. I saw them *now* even more unequivocally than I beheld them *then*. The teeth! The teeth! They were here, and there, and everywhere, and visibly and palpably before me; long, narrow, and excessively white, with the pale lips writhing about them, and in the very moment of their first terrible development. Then came the full fury of my monomania, and I struggled in vain against its strange and irresistible influence. In the multiplied objects of the external world, I had no thoughts but for the teeth. For these I longed with a frenzied desire. All other matters and all different interests became absorbed in their single contemplation. They—they alone were present to the mental eye, and they, in their sole individuality, became the essence of my mental life. I held them in every light. I turned them in every attitude. I surveyed their characteristics. I dwelt upon their peculiarities. I pondered upon their conformation. I mused upon the alteration in their nature. I shuddered as I assigned to them, in imagination, a sensitive and sentient power and, even when unassisted by the lips, a capability of moral expression. Of Mlle Salle, it has been well said, *"Que tous ses pas etaient des sentiments,"** and of

*"That all her actions were from emotions."

Berenice I more seriously believed *que toutes ses dents etaient des idées. Des idées!** Ah, here was the idiotic thought that destroyed me! *Des idées*—ah, *therefore* it was that I coveted them so madly! I felt that their possession alone could ever restore me to peace, in giving me back to reason.

And the evening closed in upon me thus—and then the darkness came and tarried and went—and the day again dawned—and the mists of a second night were now gathering around—and still I sat motionless in that solitary room—and still I sat buried in meditation—and still the *phantasma* of the teeth maintained its terrible ascendancy as, with the most vivid and hideous distinctness, it floated about amid the changing lights and shadows of the chamber. At length there broke in upon my dreams a cry as of horror and dismay, and thereunto, after a pause, succeeded the sound of troubled voices, intermingled with many low moanings of sorrow or of pain. I arose from my seat and, throwing open one of the doors of the library, saw standing out in the antechamber a servant maiden, all in tears, who told me that Berenice was no more! She had been seized with epilepsy in the early morning, and now, at the closing in of the night, the grave was ready for its tenant, and all the preparations for the burial had been completed.

I found myself sitting in the library and again sitting there alone. It seemed that I had newly awakened from a confused and exciting dream. I knew that it was now midnight, and I was well aware that since the setting of the sun Berenice had been interred. But of that dreary period which intervened, I had no positive, at least no definite, comprehension. Yet its memory was replete with

*"That her teeth were full of ideas. Of ideas!"

horror—horror more horrible from being vague and terror more terrible from ambiguity. It was a fearful page in the record of my existence, written all over with dim and hideous and unintelligible recollections. I strived to decipher them but in vain; while, ever and anon, like the spirit of a departed sound, the shrill and piercing shriek of a female voice seemed to be ringing in my ears. I had done a deed—what was it? I asked myself the question aloud, and the whispering echoes of the chamber answered me: *"What was it?"*

On the table beside me burned a lamp, and near it lay a little box. It was of no remarkable character, and I had seen it frequently before, for it was the property of the family physician; but how came it *there* upon my table, and why did I shudder in regarding it? These things were in no manner to be accounted for, and my eyes at length dropped to the open pages of a book and to a sentence underscored therein. The words were the singular but simple ones of the poet, Ebn Zaiat: *"Dicebant mihi sodales, 'Si sepulchrum amica visitarem, curas meas aliquantulum fore levatas.'* "* Why, then, as I perused them, did the hairs of my head erect themselves on end and the blood of my body become congealed within my veins?

There came a light tap at the library door—and, pale as the tenant of a tomb, a menial entered upon tiptoe. His looks were wild with terror, and he spoke to me in a voice tremulous, husky, and very low. What said he? Some broken sentences I heard. He told of a wild cry disturbing the silence of the night—of the gathering together of the household—of a search in the direction of the sound; and then his tones grew thrillingly distinct as he whispered to me of a violated grave—of a disfigured body, enshrouded

---

*"My companion said to me, 'If as a friend I should visit the grave, my worries would be a little bit relieved.' "

yet still breathing—still palpitating—*still alive.*

He pointed to my garments; they were muddy and clotted with gore. I spoke not, and he took me gently by the hand; it was indented with the impress of human nails. He directed my attention to some object against the wall. I looked at it for some minutes. It was a spade. With a shriek, I bounded to the table and grasped the box that lay upon it. But I could not force it open, and, in my tremor, it slipped from my hands and fell heavily and burst into pieces. And from it, with a rattling sound, there rolled out some instruments of dental surgery, intermingled with thirty-two small, white, and ivory-looking substances that were scattered to and fro about the floor.

The Fall of the House of Usher

DURING THE WHOLE of a dull, dark, and soundless day in the autumn of the year, when the clouds hung oppressively low in the heavens, I had been passing alone, on horseback, through a singularly dreary tract of country and at length found myself, as the shades of evening drew on, within view of the melancholy House of Usher. I know not how it was—but, with the first glimpse of the building, a sense of insufferable gloom pervaded my spirit. I say insufferable, for the feeling was unrelieved by any of that half-pleasurable, because poetic, sentiment with which the mind usually receives even the sternest natural images of the desolate or terrible. I looked upon the scene before me—upon the mere house and the simple landscape features of the domain—upon the bleak walls—upon the vacant, eyelike windows—upon a few rank sedges—and upon a few white trunks of decayed trees—with an utter depression of soul, which I can compare to no earthly sensation more properly than to the afterdream of the reveler upon opium—the bitter lapse into everyday life—the hideous dropping of the veil. There was an iciness, a sinking, a sickening of the heart—an unredeemed dreariness of thought, which no goading of the imagination could torture into aught of the sublime.

What was it—I paused to think—what was it that so unnerved me in the contemplation of the House of Usher?

It was a mystery all insoluble; nor could I grapple with the shadowy fancies that crowded upon me as I pondered. I was forced to fall back upon the unsatisfactory conclusion that while, beyond doubt, there *are* combinations of very simple natural objects which have the power of thus affecting us, still the analysis of this power lies among considerations beyond our depth. It was possible, I reflected, that a mere different arrangement of the particulars of the scene, of the details of the picture, would be sufficient to modify or perhaps to annihilate its capacity for sorrowful impression; and, acting upon this idea, I reined my horse to the precipitous brink of a black and lurid tarn that lay in unruffled luster by the dwelling, and gazed down—but with a shudder more thrilling than before—upon the remodeled and inverted images of the gray sedge and the ghastly tree stems and the vacant and eyelike windows.

Nevertheless, in this mansion of gloom I now proposed to myself a sojourn of some weeks. Its proprietor, Roderick Usher, had been one of my boon companions in boyhood, but many years had elapsed since our last meeting. A letter, however, had lately reached me in a distant part of the country—a letter from him—which, in its wildly importunate nature, had admitted of no other than a personal reply. The MS gave evidence of nervous agitation. The writer spoke of acute bodily illness—of a mental disorder which oppressed him—and of an earnest desire to see me, as his best, and indeed his only, personal friend, with a view of attempting, by the cheerfulness of my society, some alleviation of his malady. It was the manner in which all this, and much more, was said—it was the apparent *heart* that went with his request—which allowed me no room for hesitation, and I accordingly obeyed what I still considered a singular summons.

Although, as boys, we had been even intimate associates, yet I really knew little of my friend. His reserve had been always excessive and habitual. I was aware, however, that his very ancient family had been noted, time out of mind, for a peculiar sensibility of temperament, displaying itself, through long ages, in many works of exalted art and manifested of late in repeated deeds of munificent yet unobtrusive charity as well as in a passionate devotion to the intricacies, perhaps even more than to the orthodox and easily recognizable beauties, of musical science. I had learned, too, the very remarkable fact that the stem of the Usher race, all time-honored as it was, had put forth at no period any enduring branch; in other words, the entire family lay in the direct line of descent and had always, with very trifling and very temporary variation, so lain. It was this deficiency I considered while running over in thought the perfect keeping of the character of the premises with the accredited character of the people and while speculating upon the possible influence which the one, in the long lapse of centuries, might have exercised upon the other. It was this deficiency, perhaps of collateral issue, and the consequent undeviating transmission, from sire to son, of the patrimony with the name, which had at length so identified the two as to merge the original title of the estate in the quaint and equivocal appellation of the "House of Usher"—an appellation which seemed to include, in the minds of the peasantry who used it, both the family and the family mansion.

I have said that the sole effect of my somewhat childish experiment—that of looking down within the tarn—had been to deepen the first singular impression. There can be no doubt that the consciousness of the rapid increase of my superstition—for why should I not so term it?—served mainly to accelerate the increase itself. Such, I have long known, is the paradoxical law of all sentiments having terror as a basis; and it might have been for this reason only that, when I again uplifted my eyes to the house itself from its image in the pool, there grew in my mind a strange fancy—a fancy so ridiculous, indeed, that I but mention it to show the vivid force of the sensations which oppressed me. I had so worked upon my imagination as really to believe that about the whole mansion and domain there hung an atmosphere peculiar to themselves and their immediate vicinity—an atmosphere which had no affinity with the air of heaven but which had reeked up from the decayed trees and the gray wall and the silent tarn—a pestilent and mystic vapor, sluggish, faintly discernible, and leaden-hued.

Shaking off from my spirit what *must* have been a dream, I scanned more narrowly the real aspect of the building. Its principal feature seemed to be that of excessive antiquity. The discoloration of ages had been great. Minute fungi overspread the whole exterior, hanging in a fine-tangled webwork from the eaves. Yet all this was apart from any extraordinary dilapidation. No portion of the masonry had fallen, and there appeared to be a wild inconsistency between its still perfect adaptation of parts and the crumbling condition of the individual stones. In this, there was much that reminded me of the spacious totality of old woodwork which has rotted for long years in some neglected vault with no disturbance from the breath of the external air. Beyond this indication of extensive decay, however, the fabric gave little token of instability. Perhaps the eye of a scrutinizing observer might have discovered a barely perceptible fissure, which, extending from the roof of the building in front, made its way down the wall in a zigzag direction, until it became lost in the sullen waters of the tarn.

Noticing these things, I rode over a short causeway to the house. A servant in waiting took my horse, and I entered the Gothic archway of the hall. A valet, of stealthy step, thence conducted me in silence through many dark and intricate passages in my progress to the studio of his master. Much that I encountered on the way contributed, I know not how, to heighten the vague sentiments of which I have already spoken. While the objects around me—the carvings of the ceilings, the somber tapestries of the walls, the ebon blackness of the floors, and the phantasmagoric armorial trophies, which rattled as I strode—were but matters to which, or to such as which, I had been accustomed from my infancy—while I hesitated not to acknowledge how familiar was all this—I still wondered to find how unfamiliar were the fancies which ordinary images were stirring up. On one of the staircases I met the physician of the family. His countenance, I thought, wore a mingled expression of low cunning and perplexity. He accosted me with trepidation and passed on. The valet now threw open a door and ushered me into the presence of his master.

The room in which I found myself was very large and lofty. The windows were long, narrow, and pointed, and at so vast a distance from the black oaken floor as to be altogether inaccessible from within. Feeble gleams of encrimsoned light made their way through the trellised panes and served to render sufficiently distinct the more prominent objects around; the eye, however, struggled in vain to reach the remoter angles of the chamber or the recesses of the vaulted and fretted ceiling. Dark draperies hung upon the walls. The general furniture was profuse, comfortless, antique, and tattered. Many books and musical instruments lay scattered about but failed to give any vitality to the scene. I felt that I breathed an atmosphere of sorrow. An air of stern, deep, and irredeemable gloom hung over and pervaded all.

Upon my entrance, Usher arose from a sofa on which he had been lying at full length and greeted me with a vivacious warmth which had much in it, I at first thought, of an overdone cordiality—of the constrained effort of the *ennuyé* man of the world. A glance, however, at his countenance convinced me of his perfect sincerity. We sat down, and for some moments, while he spoke not, I gazed upon him with a feeling half of pity, half of awe. Surely man had never before so terribly altered, in so brief a period, as had Roderick Usher! It was with difficulty that I could bring myself to admit the identity of the wan being before me with the companion of my early boyhood. Yet the character of his face had been at all times remarkable. A cadaverousness of complexion; an eye large, liquid, and luminous beyond comparison; lips somewhat thin and very pallid, but of a surpassingly beautiful curve; a nose of a delicate Hebrew model, but with a breadth of nostril unusual in similar formations; a finely molded chin, speaking, in its want of prominence, of a want of moral energy; hair of a more than weblike softness and tenuity. These features, with an inordinate expansion above the regions of the temple, made up altogether a countenance not easily to be forgotten. And now, in the mere exaggeration of the prevailing character of these features and of the expression they were wont to convey lay so much of change that I doubted to whom I spoke. The now ghastly pallor of the skin and the now miraculous luster of the eye, above all things, startled and even awed me. The silken hair, too, had been suffered to grow all unheeded, and as, in its wild, gossamer texture, it floated rather than fell about the face, I could not, even with effort, connect its arabesque expression with any idea of simple humanity.

In the manner of my friend, I was at once struck with an incoherence—an inconsistency—and I soon found this to arise from a series of feeble and futile struggles to overcome an habitual trepidation—an excessive nervous agitation. For something of this nature I had indeed been prepared, no less by his letter than by reminiscences of certain boyish traits and by conclusions deduced from his peculiar physical conformation and temperament. His action was alternately vivacious and sullen. His voice varied rapidly from a tremulous indecision (when the animal spirits seemed utterly in abeyance) to that species of energetic conciseness—that abrupt, weighty, unhurried, and hollow-sounding enunciation—that leaden, self-balanced, and perfectly modulated guttural utterance which may be observed in the lost drunkard or in the irreclaimable eater of opium, during the periods of his most intense excitement.

It was thus that he spoke of the object of my visit, of his earnest desire to see me, and of the solace he expected me to afford him. He entered at some length into what he conceived to be the nature of his malady. It was, he said, a constitutional and a family evil and one for which he despaired to find a remedy—a mere nervous affection, he immediately added, which would undoubtedly soon pass off. It displayed itself in a host of unnatural sensations. Some of these, as he detailed them, interested and bewildered me, although perhaps the terms and the general manner of the narration had their weight. He suffered much from a morbid acuteness of the senses; the most insipid food was alone endurable; he could wear only garments of certain texture; the odors of all flowers were oppressive; his eyes were tortured by even a faint light; and there were but peculiar sounds, and these from stringed instruments, which did not inspire him with horror.

To an anomalous species of terror, I found him a bounden slave. "I shall perish," said he, "I *must* perish in this deplorable folly. Thus, thus, and not otherwise, shall I be lost. I dread the events of the future, not in themselves but in their results. I shudder at the thought of any, even the most trivial, incident which may operate upon this intolerable agitation of soul. I have indeed no abhorrence of danger, except in its absolute effect—in terror. In this unnerved—in this pitiable—condition, I feel that the period will sooner or later arrive when I must abandon life and reason together in some struggle with the grim phantasm, Fear."

I learned, moreover, at intervals and through broken and equivocal hints, another singular feature of his mental condition. He was enchained by certain superstitious impressions in regard to the dwelling which he tenanted, and whence, for many years, he had never ventured forth —in regard to an influence whose supposititious force was conveyed in terms too shadowy here to be restated—an influence which some peculiarities in the mere form and substance of his family mansion had, by dint of long sufferance, he said, obtained over his spirit—an effect which the physique of the gray walls and turrets and of the dim tarn into which they all looked down had at length brought about upon the morale of his existence.

He admitted, however, although with hesitation, that much of the peculiar gloom which thus afflicted him could be traced to a more natural and far more palpable origin—to the severe and long continued illness—indeed to the evidently approaching dissolution—of a tenderly beloved sister, his sole companion for long years, his last and only relative on earth. Her decease, he said with a bitterness which I can never forget, would leave him (him, the hopeless and the frail) the last of the ancient race of the Ushers. While he spoke, the lady Madeline (for so was she called) passed slowly through a remote part of the apartment and, without having noticed my presence, disappeared. I regarded her with an utter astonishment not unmingled with dread—and yet I found it impossible to account for such feelings. A sensation of stupor oppressed me as my eyes followed her retreating steps. When a door at length closed upon her, my glance sought instinctively and eagerly the countenance of the brother—but he had buried his face in his hands, and I could only perceive that a far more than ordinary wanness had overspread the emaciated fingers through which trickled many passionate tears.

The disease of the lady Madeline had long baffled the skill of her physicians. A settled apathy, a gradual wasting away of the person, and frequent, although transient, affections of a partially cataleptical character were the unusual diagnosis. Hitherto she had steadily borne up against the pressure of her malady and had not betaken herself finally to bed, but, on the closing in of the evening of my arrival at the house, she succumbed (as her brother told me at night with inexpressible agitation) to the prostrating power of the destroyer, and I learned that the glimpse I had obtained of her person would thus probably be the last I should obtain of her while she lived.

For several days ensuing, her name was unmentioned by either Usher or myself, and during this period I was busied in earnest endeavors to alleviate the melancholy of my friend. We painted and read together, or I listened, as if in a dream, to the wild improvisations of his speaking guitar. And thus, as a closer and still closer intimacy admitted me more unreservedly into the recesses of his spirit, the more bitterly did I perceive the futility of all attempts at cheering a mind from which darkness, as if an inherent

positive quality, poured forth upon all objects of the moral and physical universe in one unceasing radiation of gloom.

I shall ever bear about me a memory of the many solemn hours I thus spent alone with the master of the House of Usher. Yet I should fail in any attempt to convey an idea of the exact character of the studies or of the occupations in which he involved me or led me the way. An excited and highly distempered ideality threw a sulfurous luster over all. His long, improvised dirges will ring forever in my ears. Among other things, I hold painfully in mind a certain singular perversion and amplification of the wild air of the last waltz of Von Weber. From the paintings over which his elaborate fancy brooded, which grew, touch by touch, into vaguenesses at which I shuddered the more thrillingly because I shuddered knowing not why—from these paintings (vivid as their images now are before me) I would in vain endeavor to educe more than a small portion which should lie within the compass of merely written words. By the utter simplicity, by the nakedness of his designs, he arrested and overawed attention. If ever mortal painted an idea, that mortal was Roderick Usher. For me, at least—in the circumstances then surrounding me—there arose out of the pure abstractions which the hypochondriac contrived to throw upon his canvas an intensity of intolerable awe, no shadow of which felt I ever yet in the contemplation of the certainly glowing yet too concrete reveries of Fuseli.

One of the phantasmagoric conceptions of my friend, partaking not so rigidly of the spirit of abstraction, may be shadowed forth, although feebly, in words. A small picture presented the interior of an immensely long and rectangular vault or tunnel, with low walls, smooth, white, and without interruption or device. Certain accessory points of the design served well to convey the idea that this excavation lay at an exceeding depth below the surface of the earth. No outlet was observed in any portion of its vast extent, and no source of light was discernible, yet a flood of intense rays rolled throughout and bathed the whole in a ghastly and inappropriate splendor.

I have just spoken of that morbid condition of the auditory nerve, which rendered all music intolerable to the sufferer, with the exception of certain effects of stringed instruments. It was, perhaps, the narrow limits to which he thus confined himself upon the guitar which gave birth, in great measure, to the fantastic character of his performances. But the fervid *facility* of his *impromptus* could not be so accounted for. They must have been and were, in the notes as well as in the words of his wild fantasias (for he not unfrequently accompanied himself with rhymed verbal improvisations), the result of that intense mental collectedness and concentration to which I have previously alluded as observable only in particular moments of the highest artificial excitement. The words of one of these rhapsodies I have easily remembered. I was perhaps the more forcibly impressed with it as he gave it, because, in the under, or mystic, current of its meaning, I fancied that I perceived, and for the first time, a full consciousness on the part of Usher of the tottering of his lofty reason upon her throne. The verses, which were entitled "The Haunted Palace," ran very nearly, if not accurately, thus:

In the greenest of our valleys,
  By good angels tenanted,
Once a fair and stately palace—
  Radiant palace—reared its head.
In the monarch Thought's dominion
  It stood there!
Never seraph spread a pinion
  Over fabric half so fair.

Banners yellow, glorious, golden,
  On its roof did float and flow;
(This—all this—was in the olden
  Time long ago.)
And every gentle air that dallied,
  In that sweet day,
Along the ramparts plumed and pallid,
  A winged odor went away.

Wanderers in that happy valley
  Through two luminous windows saw
Spirits moving musically
  To a lute's well-tunéd law,
Round about a throne, where sitting
  (Porphyrogene!)
In state his glory well befitting,
  The ruler of the realm was seen.

And all with pearl and ruby glowing
  Was the fair palace door,
Through which came flowing, flowing, flowing,
  And sparkling evermore,
A troop of Echoes, whose sweet duty
  Was but to sing,
In voices of surpassing beauty,
  The wit and wisdom of their king.

But evil things, in robes of sorrow,
  Assailed the monarch's high estate;
(Ah, let us mourn, for never morrow
  Shall dawn upon him, desolate!)
And round about his home, the glory
  That blushed and bloomed
Is but a dim-remembered story
  Of the old time entombed.

And travelers now within that valley,
  Through the red-lighted windows, see
Vast forms that move fantastically
  To a discordant melody;
While, like a rapid, ghastly river,
  Through the pale door,
A hideous throng rush out forever,
  And laugh—but smile no more.

I well remember that suggestions arising from this ballad led us into a train of thought wherein there became manifest an opinion of Usher's, which I mention not so much on account of its novelty (for other men have thought thus) as on account of the pertinacity with which he maintained it. This opinion, in its general form, was that of the sentience of all vegetable things. But in his disordered fancy, the idea had assumed a more daring character and trespassed, under certain conditions, upon the kingdom of inorganization. I lack words to express the full extent or the earnest *abandon* of his persuasion. His belief, however, was connected (as I have previously hinted) with the gray stones of the home of his forefathers. The conditions of the sentience had been here, he imagined, fulfilled in the method of collocation of these stones—in the order of their arrangement as well as in that of the many fungi which overspread them and of the decayed trees which stood around—above all, in the long undisturbed endurance of this arrangement and in its reduplication in the still waters of the tarn. Its evidence—the evidence of the sentience—was to be seen, he said (and I here started as he spoke), in the gradual yet certain condensation of an atmosphere of their own about the waters and the walls. The result was discoverable, he added, in that silent yet importunate and terrible influence which for centuries had molded the destinies of his family and which made *him* what I now saw him—what he was. Such opinions need no comment, and I will make none.

Our books—the books which for years had formed no small portion of the mental existence of the invalid—were, as might be supposed, in strict keeping with this character of phantasm. We pored together over such works as the *Ververt et Chartreuse* of Gresset; the *Belphegor* of

Machiavelli; the *Heaven and Hell* of Swedenborg; the *Subterranean Voyage of Nicholas Klimm* by Holberg; the *Chiromancy* of Robert Flud, of Jean d'Indaginé, and of De La Chambre; the *Journey into the Blue Distance* of Tieck; and the *City of the Sun* of Campanella. One favorite volume was a small octavo edition of the *Directorium Inquisitorium* by the Dominican Eymeric de Gironne, and there were passages in Pomponius Mela about the old African satyrs and egipans, over which Usher would sit dreaming for hours. His chief delight, however, was found in the perusal of an exceedingly rare and curious book in quarto Gothic—the manual of a forgotten church, bearing the title *Vigiliae Mortuorum secundum Chorum Ecclesiae Maguntinae.*

I could not help thinking of the wild ritual of this work and its probable influence upon the hypochondriac when, one evening, having informed me abruptly that the lady Madeline was no more, he stated his intention of preserving her corpse for a fortnight (previously to its final interment) in one of the numerous vaults within the main walls of the building. The worldly reason, however, assigned for this singular proceeding was one which I did not feel at liberty to dispute. The brother had been led to his resolution (so he told me) by consideration of the unusual character of the malady of the deceased, of certain obtrusive and eager inquiries on the part of her medical men, and of the remote and exposed situation of the burial ground of the family. I will not deny that when I called to mind the sinister countenance of the doctor whom I met upon the staircase on the day of my arrival at the house, I had no desire to oppose what I regarded as harmless and by no means an unnatural precaution.

At the request of Usher, I personally aided him in the arrangements for the temporary entombment. The body having been encoffined, we two alone bore it to its rest. The vault in which we placed it (and which had been so long unopened that our torches, half smothered in its oppressive atmosphere, gave us little opportunity for investigation) was small, damp, and entirely without means of admission for light, lying at great depth immediately beneath that portion of the building in which was my own sleeping apartment. It had been used, apparently in remote feudal times, for the worst purposes of a donjon keep and in later days as a place of deposit for powder or some other highly combustible substance, as a portion of its floor and the whole interior of a long archway through which we reached it were carefully sheathed with copper. The door, of massive iron, had been also similarly protected. Its immense weight caused an unusually sharp grating sound as it moved upon its hinges.

Having deposited our mournful burden upon tressels within this region of horror, we partially turned aside the yet unscrewed lid of the coffin and looked upon the face of the tenant. A striking similitude between the brother and sister now first arrested my attention, and Usher, divining perhaps my thoughts, murmured out some few words from which I learned that the deceased and he had been twins and that sympathies of a scarcely intelligible nature had always existed between them. Our glances, however, rested not long upon the dead, for we could not regard her unawed. The disease which had thus entombed the lady in the maturity of youth had left, as usual in all maladies of a strictly cataleptical character, the mockery of a faint blush upon the bosom and the face and that suspiciously lingering smile upon the lip which is so terrible in death.

We replaced and screwed down the lid and, having secured the door of iron, made our way with toil into the scarcely less gloomy apartments of the upper portion of the house.

And now, some days of bitter grief having elapsed, an observable change came over the features of the mental disorder of my friend. His ordinary manner had vanished. His ordinary occupations were neglected or forgotten. He roamed from chamber to chamber with hurried, unequal, and objectless step. The pallor of his countenance had assumed, if possible, a more ghastly hue—but the luminousness of his eye had utterly gone out. The once occasional huskiness of his tone was heard no more, and a tremulous quaver, as if of extreme terror, habitually characterized his utterance. There were times, indeed, when I thought his unceasingly agitated mind was laboring with some oppressive secret, to divulge which he struggled for the necessary courage. At times, again, I was obliged to resolve all into the mere inexplicable vagaries of madness, for I beheld him gazing upon vacancy for long hours in an attitude of the profoundest attention, as if listening to some imaginary sound. It was no wonder that his condition terrified—that it infected—me. I felt creeping upon me, by slow yet certain degrees, the wild influences of his own fantastic yet impressive superstitions.

It was especially upon retiring to bed late in the night of the seventh or eighth day after the placing of the lady Madeline within the donjon that I experienced the full power of such feelings. Sleep came not near my couch—while the hours waned and waned away. I struggled to reason off the nervousness which had dominion over me. I endeavored to believe that much, if not all, of what I felt was due to the bewildering influence of the gloomy furniture of the room—of the dark and tattered draperies, which, tortured into motion by the breath of a rising tempest, swayed fitfully to and fro upon the walls and rustled uneasily about the decorations of the bed. But my efforts were fruitless. An irrepressible tremor gradually pervaded my frame, and at length there sat upon my very heart an incubus of utterly causeless alarm. Shaking this off with a gasp and a struggle, I uplifted myself upon the pillows and, peering earnestly within the intense darkness of the chamber, hearkened—I know not why, except that an instinctive spirit prompted me—to certain low and indefinite sounds which came, through the pauses of the storm, at long intervals, I knew not whence. Overpowered by an intense sentiment of horror, unaccountable yet unendurable, I threw on my clothes with haste (for I felt that I should sleep no more during the night) and endeavored to arouse myself from the pitiable condition into which I had fallen by pacing to and fro through the apartment.

I had taken but few turns in this manner, when a light step on an adjoining staircase arrested my attention. I presently recognized it as that of Usher. In an instant afterward, he rapped with a gentle touch at my door and entered, bearing a lamp. His countenance was, as usual, cadaverously wan—but, moreover, there was a species of mad hilarity in his eyes—an evidently restrained *hysteria* in his whole demeanor. His air appalled me—but anything was preferable to the solitude which I had so long endured, and I even welcomed his presence as a relief.

"And you have not seen it?" he said abruptly, after having stared about him for some moments in silence. "You have not then seen it? But, stay! You shall." Thus speaking, and having carefully shaded his lamp, he hurried to one of the casements and threw it freely open to the storm.

The impetuous fury of the entering gust nearly lifted us from our feet. It was indeed a tempestuous yet sternly beautiful night and one wildly singular in its terror and its beauty. A whirlwind had apparently collected its force in our vicinity, for there were frequent and violent alterations in the direction of the wind, and the exceeding density of the clouds (which hung so low as to press upon the turrets of the house) did not prevent our perceiving the lifelike velocity with which they flew, careering from all points against each other, without passing away into the distance.

I say that even their exceeding density did not prevent our perceiving this—yet we had no glimpse of the moon or stars, nor was there any flashing forth of the lightning. But the undersurfaces of the huge masses of agitated vapor as well as all terrestrial objects immediately around us were glowing in the unnatural light of a faintly luminous and distinctly visible gaseous exhalation, which hung about and enshrouded the mansion.

"You must not—you shall not—behold this!" said I shudderingly to Usher as I led him with a gentle violence from the window to a seat. "These appearances which bewilder you are merely electrical phenomena not uncommon, or it may be that they have their ghastly origin in the rank miasma of the tarn. Let us close this casement; the air is chilling and dangerous to your frame. Here is one of your favorite romances. I will read, and you shall listen; and so we will pass away this terrible night together."

The antique volume which I had taken up was the *Mad Trist* of Sir Launcelot Canning, but I had called it a favorite of Usher's more in sad jest than in earnest, for, in truth, there is little in its uncouth and unimaginative prolixity which could have had interest for the lofty and spiritual ideality of my friend. It was, however, the only book immediately at hand, and I indulged a vague hope that the excitement which now agitated the hypochondriac might find relief (for the history of mental disorder is full of similar anomalies) even in the extremeness of the folly which I should read. Could I have judged, indeed, by the wild, overstrained air of vivacity with which he hearkened, or apparently hearkened, to the words of the tale, I might well have congratulated myself upon the success of my design.

I had arrived at that well-known portion of the story where Ethelred, the hero of the Trist, having sought in vain for peaceable admission into the dwelling of the hermit, proceeds to make good an entrance by force. Here, it will be remembered, the words of the narrative run thus:

> "And Ethelred, who was by nature of a doughty heart, and who was now mighty withal, on account of the powerfulness of the wine which he had drunken, waited no longer to hold parley with the hermit, who in sooth was of an obstinate and maliceful turn, but, feeling the rain upon his shoulders and fearing the rising of the tempest, uplifted his mace outright, and with blows made quickly room in the plankings of the door for his gauntleted hand; and now pulling therewith sturdily, he so cracked and ripped and tore all asunder that the noise of the dry and hollow-sounding wood alarmed and reverberated throughout the forest."

At the termination of this sentence, I started and for a moment paused, for it appeared to me (although I at once concluded that my excited fancy had deceived me) that from some very remote portion of the mansion there came indistinctly to my ears what might have been, in its exact similarity of character, the echo (but a stifled and dull one, certainly) of the very cracking and ripping sound which Sir Launcelot had so particularly described. It was, beyond doubt, the coincidence alone which had arrested my attention, for, amid the rattling of the sashes of the casements and the ordinary commingled noises of the still increasing storm, the sound in itself had nothing surely which should have interested or disturbed me. I continued the story:

> "But the good champion Ethelred, now entering within the door, was soon enraged and amazed to perceive no signal of the maliceful hermit; but in the stead thereof, a dragon of a scaly and prodigious demeanor and of a fiery tongue, which sate in guard before a palace of gold, with a floor of silver; and upon the wall there hung a shield of shining brass with this legend enwritten—
>
> Who entereth herein, a conqueror hath bin;
> Who slayeth the dragon, the shield he shall win.
>
> And Ethelred uplifted his mace and struck upon the head of the dragon, which fell before him and gave up his pesty breath with a shriek so horrid and harsh and withal so piercing that Ethelred had fain to close his ears with his hands against the dreadful noise of it, the like whereof was never before heard."

Here again I paused abruptly, and now with a feeling of wild amazement—for there could be no doubt whatever that in this instance I did actually hear (although from what direction it proceeded, I found it impossible to say) a low and apparently distant, but harsh, protracted, and most unusual screaming or grating sound—the exact counterpart of what my fancy had already conjured up for the dragon's unnatural shriek as described by the romancer.

Oppressed, as I certainly was upon the occurrence of this second and most extraordinary coincidence, by a thousand conflicting sensations, in which wonder and extreme terror were predominate, I still retained sufficient presence of mind to avoid exciting by any observation the sensitive nervousness of my companion. I was by no means certain that he had noticed the sounds in question, although assuredly a strange alteration had during the last few minutes taken place in his demeanor. From a position fronting my own, he had gradually brought round his chair so as to sit with his face to the door of the chamber; and thus I could but partially perceive his features, although I saw that his lips trembled as if he were murmuring inaudibly. His head had dropped upon his breast, yet I knew that he was not asleep, from the wide and rigid opening of the eye as I caught a glance of it in profile. The motion of his body, too, was at variance with this idea, for he rocked from side to side with a gentle yet constant and uniform sway. Having rapidly taken notice of all this, I resumed the narrative of Sir Launcelot, which thus proceeded:

> "And now the champion, having escaped from the terrible fury of the dragon, bethinking himself of the brazen shield and of the breaking up of the enchantment which was upon it, removed the carcass from out of the way before him and approached valorously over the silver pavement of the castle to where the shield was upon the wall, which in sooth tarried not for his full coming but fell down at his feet upon the silver floor with a mighty, great, and terrible ringing sound."

No sooner had these syllables passed my lips than—as if a shield of brass had indeed at the moment fallen heavily upon a floor of silver—I became aware of a distinct hollow, metallic, and clangorous, yet apparently muffled, reverberation. Completely unnerved, I leaped to my feet, but the measured rocking movement of Usher was undisturbed. I rushed to the chair in which he sat. His eyes were bent fixedly before him, and throughout his whole countenance there reigned a stony rigidity. But as I placed my hand upon his shoulder, there came a strong shudder over his whole person; a sickly smile quivered about his lips, and I saw that he spoke in a low, hurried, and gibbering murmur, as if unconscious of my presence. Bending closely over him, I at length drank in the hideous import of his words.

"Not hear it— Yes, I hear it and *have* heard it. Long—long—long—many minutes, many hours, many days have I heard it—yet I dared not—oh, pity me, miserable wretch that I am!—I dared not—I *dared* not speak! *We have put her living in the tomb!* Said I not that my senses were acute? I *now* tell you that I heard her first feeble movements in the hollow coffin. I heard them—many, many days ago—yet I dared not—*I dared not speak!* And now—tonight—Ethelred—ha! ha!—the breaking of the hermit's door, and the death cry of the dragon, and the clangor of the shield! Say, rather, the rending of her coffin, and the grating of the iron hinges of her prison, and her struggles within the coppered archway of the vault. O whither shall I fly? Will she not be here anon? Is she not hurrying to upbraid me for my haste? Have I not heard her footstep on the stair? Do I not distinguish that heavy and horrible beating of her heart? Madman!" Here he sprang furiously to his feet and shrieked out his syllables, as if in the effort he were giving up his soul—*"Madman! I tell you that she now stands without the door!"*

As if in the superhuman energy of his utterance there had been found the potency of a spell, the huge antique panels to which the speaker pointed threw slowly back, upon the instant, their ponderous and ebony jaws. It was the work of the rushing gust—but then, without those doors, there *did* stand the lofty and enshrouded figure of the lady Madeline of Usher. There was blood upon her white robes and the evidence of some bitter struggle upon every portion of her emaciated frame. For a moment she remained, trembling and reeling to and fro, upon the threshold—then, with a low, moaning cry, fell heavily inward upon the person of her brother and in her violent and now final death agonies bore him to the floor a corpse, a victim to the terrors he had anticipated.

From that chamber and from that mansion I fled, aghast. The storm was still abroad, in all its wrath, as I found myself crossing the old causeway. Suddenly there shot along the path a wild light, and I turned to see whence a gleam so unusual could have issued, for the vast house and its shadows were alone behind me. The radiance was that of the full, setting, and blood-red moon, which now shone vividly through that once barely discernible fissure of which I have before spoken as extending from the roof of the building in a zigzag direction to the base. While I gazed, this fissure rapidly widened; there came a fierce breath of the whirlwind; the entire orb of the satellite burst at once upon my sight; my brain reeled as I saw the mighty walls rushing asunder; there was a long, tumultuous, shouting sound, like the voice of a thousand waters, and the deep and dark tarn at my feet closed sullenly and silently over the fragments of the House of Usher.

The Gold-Bug

MANY YEARS AGO I contracted an intimacy with a Mr. William Legrand. He was of an ancient Huguenot family and had once been wealthy, but a series of misfortunes had reduced him to want. To avoid the mortification consequent upon his disasters, he left New Orleans, the city of his forefathers, and took up his residence at Sullivan's Island, near Charleston, South Carolina.

This island is a very singular one. It consists of little else than the sea sand and is about three miles long. Its breadth at no point exceeds a quarter of a mile. It is separated from the mainland by a scarcely perceptible creek, oozing its way through a wilderness of reeds and slime, a favorite resort of the marsh hen. The vegetation, as might be supposed, is scant or, at least, dwarfish. No trees of any magnitude are to be seen. Near the western extremity, where Fort Moultrie stands and where are some miserable frame buildings, tenanted during summer by fugitives from Charleston dust and fever, may be found, indeed, the bristly palmetto; but the whole island, with the exception of this western point and a line of hard, white beach on the seacoast, is covered with a dense undergrowth of the sweet myrtle so much prized by the horticulturists of England. The shrub here often attains the height of fifteen or twenty feet and forms an almost impenetrable coppice, burdening the air with its fragrance.

In the inmost recesses of this coppice, not far from the eastern, or more remote, end of the island, Legrand had built himself a small hut, which he occupied when I first, by mere accident, made his acquaintance. This soon ripened into friendship—for there was much in the recluse to excite interest and esteem. I found him well educated, with unusual powers of mind, but infected with misanthropy and subject to perverse moods of alternate enthusiasm and melancholy. He had with him many books but rarely employed them. His chief amusements were gunning and fishing or sauntering along the beach and through the myrtles, in quest of shells or entomological specimens—his collection of the latter might have been envied by a Swammerdam. In these excursions he was usually accompanied by an old Negro called Jupiter, who had been manumitted before the reverses of the family but who could be induced neither by threats nor by promises to abandon what he considered his right of attendance upon the footsteps of his young "Massa Will." It is not improbable that the relatives of Legrand, conceiving him to be somewhat unsettled in intellect, had contrived to instill this obstinacy into Jupiter, with a view to the supervision and guardianship of the wanderer.

The winters in the latitude of Sullivan's Island are seldom very severe, and in the fall of the year it is a rare event indeed when a fire is considered necessary. About the middle of October, 18—, there occurred, however, a day of remarkable chilliness. Just before sunset I scrambled my way through the evergreens to the hut of my friend, whom I had not visited for several weeks—my residence being at that time in Charleston, a distance of nine miles from the island, while the facilities of passage and repassage were very far behind those of the present day. Upon reaching the hut, I rapped, as was my custom, and, getting no reply, sought for the key where I knew it was secreted, unlocked the door, and went in. A fine fire blazed upon the hearth. It was a novelty and by no means an ungrateful one. I threw off an overcoat, took an armchair by the crackling logs, and awaited patiently the arrival of my hosts.

Soon after dark, they arrived and gave me a most cordial welcome. Jupiter, grinning from ear to ear, bustled about to prepare some marsh hens for supper. Legrand was in one of his fits—how else shall I term them?—of enthusiasm. He had found an unknown bivalve, forming a new genus, and, more than this, he had hunted down and secured, with Jupiter's assistance, a scarabaeus which he believed to be totally new but in respect to which he wished to have my opinion on the morrow.

"And why not tonight?" I asked, rubbing my hands over the blaze and wishing the whole tribe of scarabaei at the devil.

"Ah, if I had only known you were here!" said Legrand. "But it's so long since I saw you, and how could I foresee that you would pay me a visit this very night of all others? As I was coming home, I met Lieutenant G——, from the fort, and, very foolishly, I lent him the bug, so it will be impossible for you to see it until the morning. Stay here tonight, and I will send Jup down for it at sunrise. It is the loveliest thing in creation!"

"What! Sunrise?"

"Nonsense! No! The bug. It is of a brilliant gold color—about the size of a large hickory nut—with two jet black spots near one extremity of the back and another, somewhat longer, at the other. The antennae are—"

"Dey ain't no tin in him, Massa Will, I keep a-tellin' on you," here interrupted Jupiter. "De bug is a goole-bug, solid, ebbery bit ob him, inside and all, sep him wing

—nebber feel half so hebby a bug in my life."

"Well, suppose it is, Jup," replied Legrand, somewhat more earnestly, it seemed to me, than the case demanded. "Is that any reason for your letting the birds burn? The color"—here he turned to me—"is really almost enough to warrant Jupiter's idea. You never saw a more brilliant metallic luster than the scales emit—but of this you cannot judge till tomorrow. In the meantime I can give you some idea of the shape." Saying this, he seated himself at a small table, on which were a pen and ink but no paper. He looked for some in a drawer but found none.

"Never mind," said he at length, "this will answer," and he drew from his waistcoat pocket a scrap of what I took to be very dirty foolscap and made upon it a rough drawing with the pen. While he did this, I retained my seat by the fire, for I was still chilly. When the design was complete, he handed it to me without rising. As I received it, a loud growl was heard, succeeded by a scratching at the door. Jupiter opened it, and a large Newfoundland, belonging to Legrand, rushed in, leaped upon my shoulders, and loaded me with caresses, for I had shown him much attention during previous visits. When his gambols were over, I looked at the paper and, to speak the truth, found myself not a little puzzled.

"Well!" I said, after contemplating it for some minutes. "This *is* a strange scarabaeus, I must confess. New to me; never saw anything like it before—unless it was a skull or a death's-head—which it more nearly resembles than anything else that has come under my observation."

"A death's-head!" echoed Legrand. "Oh—yes—well, it has something of that appearance upon paper, no doubt. The two upper black spots look like eyes, eh? And the longer one at the bottom like a mouth—and then the shape of the whole is oval."

"Perhaps so," said I, "but, Legrand, I fear you are no artist. I must wait until I see the beetle itself if I am to form any idea of its personal appearance."

"Well, I don't know," said he, a little nettled. "I draw tolerably—*should* do it, at least—have had good masters and flatter myself that I am not quite a blockhead."

"But, my dear fellow, you are joking, then," said I. "This is a very passable *skull*—indeed, I may say that it is a very *excellent* skull, according to the vulgar notions about such specimens of physiology—and your scarabaeus must be the queerest scarabaeus in the world if it resembles it. Why, we may get up a very thrilling bit of superstition upon this hint. I presume you will call the bug *Scarabaeus caput hominis* or something of that kind. There are many similar titles in the natural histories. But where are the antennae you spoke of?"

"The antennae!" said Legrand, who seemed to be getting unaccountably warm upon the subject. "I am sure you must see the antennae. I made them as distinct as they are in the original insect, and I presume that should be sufficient."

"Well, well," I said, "perhaps you have—still, I don't see them." I handed him the paper without additional remark, not wishing to ruffle his temper, but I was much surprised at the turn affairs had taken. His ill humor puzzled me—and, as for the drawing of the beetle, there were positively no antennae visible, and the whole *did* bear a very close resemblance to the ordinary cuts of a death's-head.

He received the paper very peevishly and was about to crumple it, apparently to throw it in the fire, when a casual glance at the design seemed suddenly to rivet his attention. In an instant his face grew violently red—in another as excessively pale. For some minutes he continued to scrutinize the drawing minutely where he sat. At length he arose, took a candle from the table, and proceeded to seat himself upon a sea chest in the farthest corner of the room. Here again he made an anxious examination of the paper, turning it in all directions. He said nothing, however, and his conduct greatly astonished me, yet I thought it prudent not to exacerbate the growing moodiness of his temper by any comment. Presently he took from his coat pocket a wallet, placed the paper carefully in it, and deposited both in a writing desk, which he locked. He now grew more composed in his demeanor, but his original air of enthusiasm had quite disappeared. Yet he seemed not so much sulky as abstracted. As the evening wore away, he became more and more absorbed in reverie, from which no sallies of mine could arouse him. It had been my intention to pass the night at the hut, as I had frequently done before, but, seeing my host in this mood, I deemed it proper to take leave. He did not press me to remain, but, as I departed, he shook my hand with even more than his usual cordiality.

It was about a month after this (and during the interval I had seen nothing of Legrand) when I received a visit, at Charleston, from his man, Jupiter. I had never seen the good old Negro look so dispirited, and I feared that some serious disaster had befallen my friend.

"Well, Jup," said I, "what is the matter now? How is your master?"

"Why, to speak de troof, massa, him not so berry well as mought be."

"Not well! I am truly sorry to hear it. What does he complain of?"

"Dar! Dat's it! Him nebber 'plain of nuffin—but him berry sick, for all dat."

"*Very* sick, Jupiter! Why didn't you say so at once? Is he confined to bed?"

"No, dat he ain't! He ain't 'fin'd nowhar—dat's jis whar de shoe pinch—my mind is got to be berry hebby 'bout poor Massa Will."

"Jupiter, I should like to understand what it is you are talking about. You say your master is sick. Hasn't he told you what ails him?"

"Why, massa, tain't worfwhile for to git mad 'bout de matter. Massa Will say nuffin at all ain't de matter wid him—but den what make him go 'bout looking dis here way, wid he head down and he soldiers up and as white as a gose? And den he keeps a siphon all de time—"

"Keeps a what, Jupiter?"

"Keeps a siphon wid de figgurs on de slate—de queerest figgurs I ebber did see. Ise gitten to be skeered, I tell you. Hab for to keep moughty tight eye 'pon him noovers. Todder day he gib me slip 'fore de sun up and was gone de whole ob de blessed day. I had a big stick ready-cut for to gib him deuced good beating when he did come—but Ise sich a fool dat I hadn't de heart, arter all—he look so berry poorly."

"Eh—what?—ah, yes!—upon the whole, I think you had better not be too severe with the poor fellow. Don't flog him, Jupiter—he can't very well stand it—but can you form no idea of what has occasioned this illness, or rather, this change of conduct? Has anything unpleasant happened since I saw you?"

"No, massa, dey ain't bin nuffin onpleasant *since* den —'twas *'fore* den, Ise feared—'twas de berry day you was dar."

"How? What do you mean?"

"Why, massa, I mean de bug—dar, now."

"The what?"

"De bug—I'm berry sartain dat Massa Will bin bit somewhere 'bout de head by dat goole-bug."

"And what cause have you, Jupiter, to make such a supposition?"

"Claws enuff, massa, and mouff, too. I nebber did see sich a deuced bug—he kick and he bite ebberyting what come near him. Massa Will cotch him fuss but had for to let him go 'g'in moughty quick, I tell you—den was de time he must ha' got de bite. I didn't like de look ob dat bug's mouff, myself, so I wouldn't take hold ob him wid my finger, but I cotch him wid a piece ob paper dat I found. I wrap him up in de paper and stuff piece ob it in he mouff—dat was de way."

"And you think, then, that your master was really bitten by the beetle, and that the bite made him sick?"

"I don't t'ink nuffin 'bout it—I knows it. What make him dream 'bout de goole so much, if tain't 'cause he bit by de goole-bug? Ise heered 'bout dem goole-bugs 'fore dis."

"But how do you know he dreams about gold?"

"How I know? Why, 'cause he talk 'bout it in he sleep —dat's how I knows."

"Well, Jup, perhaps you are right, but to what fortunate circumstance am I to attribute the honor of a visit from you today?"

"What de matter, massa?"

"Did you bring any message from Mr. Legrand?"

"No, massa, I bring dis here 'pissel." And here Jupiter handed me a note which ran thus:

My Dear ———,

Why have I not seen you for so long a time? I hope you have not been so foolish as to take offense at any little *brusquerie* of mine; but, no, that is improbable.

> Since I saw you I have had great cause for anxiety. I have something to tell you, yet scarcely know how to tell it or whether I should tell it at all.
>
> I have not been quite well for some days past, and poor old Jup annoys me, almost beyond endurance, by his well-meant attentions. Would you believe it? He had prepared a huge stick the other day, with which to chastise me for giving him the slip and spending the day, *solus,* among the hills on the mainland. I verily believe that my ill looks alone saved me a flogging.
>
> I have made no addition to my cabinet since we met.
>
> If you can in any way make it convenient, come over with Jupiter. *Do* come. I wish to see you *tonight* upon business of importance. I assure you that it is of the *highest* importance. Ever yours,
>
> William Legrand

There was something in the tone of this note which gave me great uneasiness. Its whole style differed materially from that of Legrand. What could he be dreaming of? What new crotchet possessed his excitable brain? What "business of the highest importance" could *he* possibly have to transact? Jupiter's account of him boded no good. I dreaded lest the continued pressure of misfortune had, at length, fairly unsettled the reason of my friend. Without a moment's hesitation, therefore, I prepared to accompany the Negro.

Upon reaching the wharf, I noticed a scythe and three spades, all apparently new, lying in the bottom of the boat in which we were to embark.

"What is the meaning of all this, Jup?" I inquired.

"Him syfe, massa, and spade."

"Very true, but what are they doing here?"

"Him de syfe and de spade what Massa Will 'sis' 'pon me buying for him in de town, and de debbil's own lot of money I had to gib for 'em."

"But what, in the name of all that is mysterious, is your

'Massa Will' going to do with scythes and spades?"

"Dat's more dan *I* knows, and debbil take me if I don't b'lieve 'tis more dan he know, too. But it's all come ob de bug."

Finding that no satisfaction was to be obtained of Jupiter, whose whole intellect seemed to be absorbed by "de bug," I now stepped into the boat and made sail. With a fair and strong breeze, we soon ran into the little cove to the northward of Fort Moultrie, and a walk of some two miles brought us to the hut. It was about three in the afternoon when we arrived. Legrand had been awaiting us in eager expectation. He grasped my hand with a nervous *empressement,* which alarmed me and strengthened the suspicions already entertained. His countenance was pale, even to ghastliness, and his deep-set eyes glared with unnatural luster. After some inquiries respecting his health, I asked him, not knowing what better to say, if he had yet obtained the scarabaeus from Lieutenant G——.

"Oh, yes," he replied, coloring violently, "I got it from him the next morning. Nothing should tempt me to part with that scarabaeus. Do you know that Jupiter is quite right about it?"

"In what way?" I asked, with a sad foreboding at heart.

"In supposing it to be a bug of *real gold.*" He said this with an air of profound seriousness, and I felt inexpressibly shocked.

"This bug is to make my fortune," he continued, with a triumphant smile, "to reinstate me in my family possessions. Is it any wonder, then, that I prize it? Since Fortune has thought fit to bestow it upon me, I have only to use it properly and I shall arrive at the gold of which it is the index. Jupiter, bring me that scarabaeus!"

"What! De bug, massa? I'd rudder not go for trouble

dat bug—you mus' git him for your own self."

Hereupon Legrand arose, with a grave and stately air, and brought me the beetle from a glass case in which it was enclosed. It was a beautiful scarabaeus and, at that time, unknown to naturalists—of course a great prize in a scientific point of view. There were two round black spots near one extremity of the back and a long one near the other. The scales were exceedingly hard and glossy, with all the appearance of burnished gold. The weight of the insect was very remarkable, and, taking all things into consideration, I could hardly blame Jupiter for his opinion respecting it; but what to make of Legrand's concordance with that opinion, I could not, for the life of me, tell.

"I sent for you," said he in a grandiloquent tone, when I had completed my examination of the beetle, "I sent for you, that I might have your counsel and assistance in furthering the views of Fate and of the bug—"

"My dear Legrand," I cried, interrupting him, "you are certainly unwell and had better use some little precautions. You shall go to bed, and I will remain with you a few days until you get over this. You are feverish and—"

"Feel my pulse," said he.

I felt it, and, to say the truth, found not the slightest indication of fever.

"But you may be ill and yet have no fever. Allow me this once to prescribe for you. In the first place, go to bed. In the next—"

"You are mistaken," he interposed. "I am as well as I can expect to be, under the excitement which I suffer. If you really wish me well, you will relieve this excitement."

"And how is this to be done?"

"Very easily. Jupiter and I are going upon an expedition into the hills upon the mainland. In this expedition, we shall need the aid of some person in whom we can confide. You are the only one we can trust. Whether we succeed or fail, the excitement which you now perceive in me will be equally allayed."

"I am anxious to oblige you in any way," I replied, "but do you mean to say that this infernal beetle has any connection with your expedition into the hills?"

"It has."

"Then, Legrand, I can become a party to no such absurd proceeding."

"I am sorry—very sorry—for we shall have to try it by ourselves."

"Try it by yourselves!" The man must surely be mad! "But stay! How long do you propose to be absent?"

"Probably all night. We shall start immediately and be back, at all events, by sunrise."

"And will you promise me, upon your honor, that when this freak of yours is over and the bug business (good God!) settled to your satisfaction, you will then return home and follow my advice implicitly, as that of your physician?"

"Yes, I promise. And now let us be off, for we have no time to lose."

With a heavy heart, I accompanied my friend. We started about four o'clock—Legrand, Jupiter, the dog, and I. Jupiter had with him the scythe and spades, the whole of which he insisted upon carrying—more through fear, it seemed to me, of trusting either of the implements within reach of his master than from any excess of industry or complaisance. His demeanor was dogged in the extreme, and "dat deuced bug" were the sole words which escaped his lips during the journey. For my own part, I had charge of a couple of dark lanterns, while Legrand contented himself with the scarabaeus, which he carried attached to the end of a bit of whipcord, twirling it to and fro with the air of a conjuror as he went. When I observed this last plain evidence of my friend's aberration of mind, I could scarcely refrain from tears. I thought it best, however, to humor his fancy, at least for the present or until I could adopt some more energetic measures with a chance of success. In the meantime I endeavored, but all in vain, to sound him in regard to the object of the expedition. Having succeeded in inducing me to accompany him, he seemed unwilling to hold conversation upon any topic of minor importance and to all my questions vouchsafed no other reply than "We shall see!"

We crossed the creek at the head of the island by means of a skiff and, ascending the high ground on the shore of the mainland, proceeded in a northwesterly direction through a tract of country excessively wild and desolate, where no trace of a human footstep was to be seen. Legrand led the way with decision, pausing only for an instant here and there to consult what appeared to be certain landmarks of his own contrivance upon a former occasion.

In this manner we journeyed for about two hours, and the sun was just setting when we entered a region infinitely more dreary than any yet seen. It was a species of tableland, near the summit of an almost inaccessible hill, densely wooded from base to pinnacle and interspersed with huge crags that appeared to lie loosely upon the soil and in many cases were prevented from precipitating themselves into valleys below merely by the support of the trees against which they reclined. Deep ravines, in various directions, gave an air of still sterner solemnity to the scene.

The natural platform to which we had clambered was thickly overgrown with brambles, through which we soon discovered that it would have been impossible to force our way but for the scythe; and Jupiter, by direction of his master, proceeded to clear for us a path to the foot of an enormously tall tulip tree which stood, with some eight or ten oaks, upon the level and far surpassed them all and all other trees which I had then ever seen in the beauty of its foliage and form, in the wide spread of its branches, and in the general majesty of its appearance. When we reached this tree, Legrand turned to Jupiter and asked him if he thought he could climb it. The old man seemed a little staggered by the question and for some moments made no reply. At length he approached the huge trunk, walked slowly around it, and examined it with minute attention. When he had completed his scrutiny, he merely said, "Yes, massa, Jup climb any tree he ebber see in he life."

"Then up with you, as soon as possible, for it will soon be too dark to see what we are about."

"How far mus' go up, massa?" inquired Jupiter.

"Get up the main trunk first, and then I will tell you which way to go—and here—stop! Take this with you."

"De bug, Massa Will? De goole-bug?" cried the Negro, drawing back in dismay. "What for mus' tote de bug way up de tree? D——n if I do!"

"If you are afraid, Jup, a great big Negro like you, to take hold of a harmless little dead beetle, why, you can carry it up by this string—but if you do not take it up with you in some way, I shall be under the necessity of breaking your head with this shovel."

"What de matter now, massa?" said Jup, evidently shamed into compliance. "Always want for to raise fuss wid old nigger. Was only funnin', anyhow. *Me* feered de bug! What I keer for de bug?" Here he cautiously took hold of the extreme end of the string and, maintaining the insect as far from his person as circumstances would permit, prepared to ascend the tree.

In youth, the tulip tree, or *Liriodendron tulipiferum,* the most magnificent of American foresters, has a trunk peculiarly smooth and often rises to a great height without lateral branches; but, in its riper age, the bark becomes gnarled and uneven, while many short limbs make their appearance on the stem. Thus the difficulty of ascension, in the present case, lay more in semblance than in reality. Embracing the huge cylinder as closely as possible with his arms and knees, seizing with his hands some projections and resting his naked toes upon others, Jupiter, after one or two narrow escapes from falling, at length wriggled himself into the first great fork and seemed to consider the whole business as virtually accomplished. The *risk* of the achievement was, in fact, now over, although the climber was some sixty or seventy feet from the ground.

"Which way mus' go now, Massa Will?" he asked.

"Keep up the largest branch—the one on this side," said Legrand. The Negro obeyed him promptly and apparently with but little trouble, ascending higher and higher, until no glimpse of his squat figure could be obtained through the dense foliage which enveloped it. Presently his voice was heard in a sort of hallo.

"How much fudder is got for go?"

"How high up are you?" asked Legrand.

"Ebber so far," replied the Negro. "Can see de sky fru de top ob de tree."

"Never mind the sky, but attend to what I say. Look down the trunk and count the limbs below you on this side. How many limbs have you passed?"

"One, two, three, four, fibe—I done pass fibe big limb, massa, 'pon dis side."

"Then go one limb higher."

In a few minutes the voice was heard again, announcing that the seventh limb was attained.

"Now, Jup," cried Legrand, evidently much excited, "I want you to work your way out upon that limb as far as you can. If you see anything strange, let me know."

By this time, what little doubt I might have entertained of my poor friend's insanity was put finally at rest. I had no alternative but to conclude him stricken with lunacy, and I became seriously anxious about getting him home. While I was pondering upon what was best to be done, Jupiter's voice was again heard.

"Mos' feered for to ventur 'pon dis limb berry far—'tis dead limb putty much all de way."

"Did you say it was a *dead* limb, Jupiter?" cried Legrand in a quavering voice.

"Yes, massa, him dead as de doornail—done up for sartain—done departed dis here life."

"What in the name of heaven shall I do?" asked Legrand, seemingly in the greatest distress.

"Do!" said I, glad of an opportunity to interpose a word. "Why, come home and go to bed. Come, now! That's a fine fellow. It's getting late, and, besides, you remember your promise."

"Jupiter," cried he, without heeding me in the least, "do you hear me?"

"Yes, Massa Will, hear you ebber so plain."

"Try the wood well, then, with your knife, and see if you think it *very* rotten."

"Him rotten, massa, sure nuff," replied the Negro in a few moments, "but not so berry rotten as mought be. Mought ventur out leetle way 'pon de limb by myself, dat's true."

"By yourself! What do you mean?"

"Why, I mean de bug. 'Tis *berry* hebby bug. S'pose I drop him down fuss, and den de limb won't break wid just de weight ob one nigger."

"You infernal scoundrel!" cried Legrand, apparently much relieved. "What do you mean by telling me such nonsense as that? As sure as you drop that beetle, I'll break your neck. Look here, Jupiter, do you hear me?"

"Yes, massa, needn't holler at poor nigger dat style."

"Well! Now, listen! If you will venture out on the limb as far as you think safe and not let go the beetle, I'll make you a present of a silver dollar as soon as you get down."

"Ise gwine, Massa Will—'deed I is," replied the Negro very promptly. "Mos' out to de end now."

"Out to the end!" here fairly screamed Legrand. "Do you say you are out to the end of that limb?"

"Soon be to de end, massa—o-o-o-o-oh! Lorgol-a-marcy! What *is* dis here 'pon de tree?"

"Well," cried Legrand, highly delighted, "what is it?"

"Why, tain't nuffin but a skull—somebody bin lef' him head up de tree, and de crows done gobble ebbery bit ob de meat off."

"A skull, you say! Very well! How is it fastened to the limb? What holds it on?"

"Sure nuff, massa, mus' look. Why, dis berry curous sarcumstance, 'pon my word—dar's a great big nail in de skull what fastens ob it onto de tree."

"Well, now, Jupiter, do exactly as I tell you—do you hear?"

"Yes, massa."

"Pay attention, then! Find the left eye of the skull."

"Hum! Hoo! Dat's good! Why, dar ain't no eye lef' at all."

"Curse your stupidity! Do you know your right hand from your left?"

"Yes, I knows dat—knows all 'bout dat—'tis my lef' hand what I chops de wood wid."

"To be sure! You are left-handed, and your left eye is

on the same side as your left hand. Now, I suppose, you can find the left eye of the skull, or the place where the left eye has been. Have you found it?"

Here was a long pause. At length the Negro asked, "Is de lef' eye ob de skull 'pon de same side as de lef' hand of de skull, too? 'Cause de skull ain't got not a bit ob a hand at all—nebber mind! I got de lef' eye now—here de lef' eye! What mus' do wid it?"

"Let the beetle drop through it, as far as the string will reach—but be careful not to let go your hold of the string."

"All dat done, Massa Will; moughty easy ting for to put de bug fru de hole—look out for him dare below!"

During this colloquy, no portion of Jupiter's person could be seen; but the beetle, which he had suffered to descend, was now visible at the end of the string and glistened, like a globe of burnished gold, in the last rays of the setting sun, some of which still faintly illumined the eminence upon which we stood. The *scarabaeus* hung quite clear of any branches, and, if allowed to fall, would have fallen at our feet. Legrand immediately took the scythe and cleared with it a circular space three or four yards in diameter, just beneath the insect, and, having accomplished this, ordered Jupiter to let go the string and come down from the tree.

Driving a peg, with great nicety, into the ground at the precise spot where the beetle fell, my friend now produced from his pocket a tape measure. Fastening one end of this at that point of the trunk of the tree which was nearest the peg, he unrolled it till it reached the peg and thence farther unrolled it, in the direction already established by the two points of the tree and the peg, for the distance of fifty feet—Jupiter clearing away the brambles with the scythe. At the spot thus attained, a second peg was driven, and, using this as a center, a rude circle, about four feet in diameter, was described. Taking now a spade himself and giving one to Jupiter and one to me, Legrand begged us to set about digging as quickly as possible.

To speak the truth, I had no especial relish for such amusement at any time and at that particular moment would most willingly have declined it, for the night was coming on, and I felt much fatigued with the exercise already taken; but I saw no mode of escape and was fearful of disturbing my poor friend's equanimity by a refusal. Could I have depended, indeed, upon Jupiter's aid, I would have had no hesitation in attempting to get the lunatic home by force; but I was too well assured of the old Negro's disposition to hope that he would assist me, under any circumstances, in a personal contest with his master. I made no doubt that the latter had been infected with some of the innumerable southern superstitions about money buried and that his fantasy had received confirmation by the finding of the scarabaeus or, perhaps, by Jupiter's obstinacy in maintaining it to be "a bug of real gold." A mind disposed to lunacy would readily be led away by such suggestions, especially if chiming in with favorite preconceived ideas—and then I called to mind the poor fellow's speech about the beetle's being the index of his fortune. Upon the whole, I was sadly vexed and puzzled, but at length I concluded to make a virtue of necessity—to dig with a good will and thus the sooner to convince the visionary, by ocular demonstration, of the fallacy of the opinions he entertained.

The lanterns having been lit, we all fell to work with a zeal worthy of a more rational cause, and as the glare fell upon our persons and implements, I could not help thinking how picturesque a group we composed and how strange and suspicious our labors must have appeared to any interloper who might have stumbled upon us.

We dug very steadily for two hours. Little was said, and our chief embarrassment lay in the yelpings of the dog, who took exceeding interest in our proceedings. He at length became so obstreperous that we grew fearful of his giving the alarm to any stragglers in the vicinity—or, rather, this was the apprehension of Legrand; for myself, I should have rejoiced at any interruption which might have enabled me to get the wanderer home. The noise was, at length, very effectually silenced by Jupiter, who, getting out of the hole with a dogged air of deliberation, tied up the brute's mouth with one of his suspenders and then returned, with a grave chuckle, to his task.

When the time mentioned had expired, we had reached a depth of five feet, and yet no signs of any treasure became manifest. A general pause ensued, and I began to hope that the farce was at an end. Legrand, however, although evidently much disconcerted, wiped his brow thoughtfully and recommenced. We had excavated the entire circle of four feet diameter, and now we slightly enlarged the limit and went to the farther depth of two feet. Still nothing appeared. The gold-seeker, whom I sincerely pitied, at length clambered from the pit, with the bitterest disappointment imprinted upon every feature, and proceeded, slowly and reluctantly, to put on his coat, which he had thrown off at the beginning of his labor. In the meantime I made no remark. Jupiter, at a signal from his master, began to gather up his tools. This done, and the dog having been unmuzzled, we turned in profound silence toward home.

We had taken perhaps a dozen steps in this direction, when, with a loud oath, Legrand strode up to Jupiter and seized him by the collar. The astonished Negro opened his eyes and mouth to the fullest extent, let fall the spades, and fell upon his knees.

"You scoundrel," said Legrand, hissing out the syllables from between his clenched teeth, "you infernal black villain! Speak, I tell you! Answer me this instant, without prevarication! Which—which is your left eye?"

"Oh, my golly, Massa Will! Ain't dis here my lef' eye for sartain?" roared the terrified Jupiter, placing his hand upon his *right* organ of vision and holding it there with a desperate pertinacity, as if in immediate dread of his master's attempt at a gouge.

"I thought so! I knew it! Hurrah!" vociferated Legrand, letting the Negro go and executing a series of curvets and caracoles, much to the astonishment of his valet, who, arising from his knees, looked mutely from his master to me and then from me to his master.

"Come! We must go back," said the latter. "The game's not up yet." And he again led the way to the tulip tree.

"Jupiter," said he, when he reached its foot, "come here! Was the skull nailed to the limb with the face outward or with the face to the limb?"

"De face was out, massa, so dat de crows could git at de eyes good, widout any trouble."

"Well, then, was it this eye or that through which you dropped the beetle?" Here Legrand touched each of Jupiter's eyes.

" 'Twas dis eye, massa—de lef' eye—jis as you tell me," and here it was his right eye that the Negro indicated.

"That will do—we must try it again."

Here my friend, about whose madness I now saw, or fancied that I saw, certain indications of method, removed the peg which marked the spot where the beetle fell to a spot about three inches to the westward of its former position. Taking, now, the tape measure from the nearest point of the trunk to the peg, as before, and continuing the extension in a straight line to the distance of fifty feet, a spot was indicated, removed by several yards from the point at which we had been digging.

Around the new position a circle, somewhat larger than in the former instance, was now described, and we again set to work with the spades. I was dreadfully weary, but, scarcely understanding what had occasioned the change in my thoughts, I felt no longer any great aversion to the labor imposed. I had become most unaccountably interested—nay, even excited. Perhaps there was something, amid all the extravagant demeanor of Legrand—some air of forethought or of deliberation which impressed me. I dug eagerly and now and then caught myself actually looking, with something that very much resembled expectation, for the fancied treasure, the vision of which had demented my unfortunate companion. At a period when such vagaries of thought most fully possessed me and when we had been at work perhaps an hour and a half, we were again interrupted by the violent howlings of the dog. His uneasiness in the first instance had been evidently but the result of playfulness or caprice, but he now assumed a bitter and serious tone. Upon Jupiter's again attempting to muzzle him, he made furious resistance and, leaping into the hole, tore up the mold frantically with his claws. In a few seconds he had uncovered a mass of human bones, forming two complete skeletons, intermingled with several buttons of metal and what appeared to be the dust of decayed woolen. One or two strokes of a spade upturned the blade of a large Spanish knife, and as we dug farther, three or four loose pieces of gold and silver coin came to light.

At the sight of these, the joy of Jupiter could scarcely be restrained, but the countenance of his master wore an air of extreme disappointment. He urged us, however, to continue our exertions, and the words were hardly uttered when I stumbled and fell forward, having caught the toe of my boot in a large ring of iron that lay half-buried in the loose earth.

We now worked in earnest, and never did I pass ten minutes of more intense excitement. During this interval, we had fairly unearthed an oblong chest of wood which, from its perfect preservation and wonderful hardness, had plainly been subjected to some mineralizing process—perhaps that of the bichloride of mercury. This box was three feet and a half long, three feet broad, and two and a half feet deep. It was firmly secured by bands of wrought iron, riveted, forming a kind of open trelliswork over the whole. On each side of the chest, near the top, were three rings of iron—six in all—by means of which a firm hold could be obtained by six persons. Our utmost united endeavors served only to disturb the coffer very slightly in its bed. We at once saw the impossibility of removing so great a weight. Luckily the sole fastenings of the lid consisted of two sliding bolts. These we drew back—trembling and panting with anxiety. In an instant, a treasure of incalculable value lay gleaming before us. As the rays of the lanterns fell within the pit, there flashed upward a glow and a glare from a confused heap of gold and jewels that absolutely dazzled our eyes.

I shall not pretend to describe the feelings with which I gazed. Amazement was, of course, predominant. Legrand appeared exhausted with excitement and spoke very few words. Jupiter's countenance wore, for some minutes, as deadly a pallor as it is possible, in the nature of things, for any Negro's visage to assume. He seemed stupefied—thunderstricken. Presently he fell upon his knees in the pit and, burying his naked arms up to the elbows in gold, let them there remain, as if enjoying the luxury of a bath.

At length, with a deep sigh, he exclaimed, as if in a soliloquy, "And dis all come ob de goole-bug? De putty goole-bug! De poor leetle goole-bug what I 'boosed in dat sabbage kind ob style! Ain't you 'shamed ob yourself, nigger? Answer me dat!"

It became necessary, at last, that I should arouse both master and valet to the expediency of removing the treasure. It was growing late, and it behooved us to make exertion, that we might get everything housed before daylight. It was difficult to say what should be done, and much time was spent in deliberation, so confused were the ideas of all. We finally lightened the box by removing two-thirds of its contents, so we were enabled, with some trouble, to raise it from the hole. The articles taken out were deposited among the brambles and the dog left to guard them, with strict orders from Jupiter neither to stir from the spot nor to open his mouth until our return. We then hurriedly made for home with the chest, reaching the hut in safety but after excessive toil, at one o'clock in the morning. Worn out as we were, it was not in human nature to do more immediately. We rested until two and had supper, starting for the hills immediately afterward, armed with three stout sacks, which, by good luck, were upon the premises. A little before four, we arrived at the pit, divided the remainder of the booty, as equally as might be, among us, and, leaving the holes unfilled, again set out for the hut, at which, for the second time, we deposited our golden burdens just as the first faint streaks of the dawn gleamed from over the treetops in the east.

We were now thoroughly broken-down, but the intense excitement of the time denied us repose. After an unquiet slumber of some three or four hours' duration, we arose, as if by preconcert, to make examination of our treasure.

The chest had been full to the brim, and we spent the

whole day and the greater part of the next night in a scrutiny of its contents. There had been nothing like order or arrangement. Everything had been heaped in promiscuously. Having assorted all with care, we found ourselves possessed of even vaster wealth than we had at first supposed. In coin, there was rather more than $450,000—estimating the value of the pieces as accurately as we could by the tables of the period. There was not a particle of silver. All was gold of antique date and of great variety—French, Spanish, and German money, with a few English guineas and some counters, of which we had never seen specimens before. There were several very large and heavy coins, so worn that we could make nothing of their inscriptions. There was no American money. The value of the jewels we found more difficulty in estimating. There were diamonds—some of them exceedingly large and fine—110 in all, and not one of them small; eighteen rubies, of remarkable brilliancy; 310 emeralds, all very beautiful; and twenty-one sapphires, with an opal. These stones had all been broken from their settings and thrown loose in the chest. The settings themselves, which we picked out from among the other gold, appeared to have been beaten up with hammers, as if to prevent identification. Besides all this, there was a vast quantity of solid gold ornaments: nearly two hundred massive finger rings and earrings; rich chains—thirty of these, if I remember—eighty-three very large and heavy crucifixes; five gold censers, of great value; a prodigious golden punch bowl, ornamented with richly chased vine leaves and bacchanalian figures; two sword handles, exquisitely embossed; and many other smaller articles which I cannot recollect. The weight of these valuables exceeded 350 pounds avoirdupois, and in this estimate I have not included 197 superb gold watches, three of the number being worth each five hundred dollars, if one. Many of them were very old and, as timekeepers, valueless—the works having suffered, more or less, from corrosion—but all were richly jeweled and in cases of great worth. We estimated the entire contents of the chest, that night, at a million and a half dollars, and, upon the subsequent disposal of the trinkets and jewels (a few being retained for our own use), it was found that we had greatly undervalued the treasure.

When at length we had concluded our examination and the intense excitement of the time had in some measure subsided, Legrand, who saw that I was dying with impatience for a solution of this most extraordinary riddle, entered into a full detail of all the circumstances connected with it.

"You remember," said he, "the night when I handed you the rough sketch I had made of the scarabaeus. You recollect also, that I became quite vexed at you for insisting that my drawing resembled a death's-head. When you first made this assertion, I thought you were jesting, but afterward I called to mind the peculiar spots on the back of the insect and admitted to myself that your remark had some little foundation in fact. Still, the sneer at my graphic powers irritated me—for I am considered a good artist—and therefore when you handed me the scrap of parchment, I was about to crumple it up and throw it angrily into the fire."

"The scrap of paper, you mean," said I.

"No, it had much of the appearance of paper, and at first I supposed it to be such, but when I came to draw upon it, I at once discovered it to be a piece of very thin parchment. It was quite dirty, you remember. Well, as I was in the very act of crumpling it up, my glance fell upon the sketch at which you had been looking, and you may imagine my astonishment when I perceived, in fact, the figure of a death's-head just where, it seemed to me, I had made the drawing of the beetle. For a moment I was too much amazed to think with accuracy. I knew that my design was very different in detail from this, although there was a certain similarity in general outline. Presently I took a candle and, seating myself at the other end of the room, proceeded to scrutinize the parchment more closely. Upon turning it over, I saw my own sketch upon the reverse, just as I had made it. My first idea, now, was mere surprise at the really remarkable similarity of outline—at the singular coincidence involved in the fact that, unknown to me, there should have been a skull upon the other side of the parchment, immediately beneath my figure of the scarabaeus, and that this skull, not only in outline but in size, should so closely resemble my drawing. I say the singularity of this coincidence absolutely stupefied me for a time. This is the usual effect of such coincidences. The mind struggles to establish a connection—a sequence of cause and effect—and, being unable to do so, suffers a species of temporary paralysis. But when I recovered from this stupor, there dawned upon me gradually a conviction which startled me even far more than the coincidence. I began distinctly, positively, to remember that there had been *no* drawing upon the parchment when I made my sketch of the scarabaeus. I became perfectly certain of this, for I recollected turning up first one side and then the other, in search of the cleanest spot. Had the skull been there then, of course I could not have failed to notice it. Here was indeed a mystery which I felt it impossible to explain, but even at that early moment there seemed to glimmer faintly, within the most remote and secret chambers of my intellect, a glowworm-like conception of that truth which last night's adventure brought to so magnificent a demonstration. I arose at once and, putting the parchment securely away, dismissed all further reflection until I should be alone.

"When you had gone and when Jupiter was fast asleep, I betook myself to a more methodical investigation of the affair. In the first place, I considered the manner in which the parchment had come into my possession. The spot where we discovered the scarabaeus was on the coast of the mainland, about a mile eastward of the island and but a short distance above high-water mark. Upon my taking hold of it, it gave me a sharp bite, which caused me to let it drop. Jupiter, with his accustomed caution, before seizing the insect, which had flown toward him, looked about him for a leaf or something of that nature by which to take hold of it. It was at this moment that his eyes and mine, also, fell upon the scrap of parchment, which I then supposed to be paper. It was lying half-buried in the sand, a corner sticking up. Near the spot where we found it, I observed the remnants of the hull of what appeared to have been a ship's longboat. The wreck seemed to have been there for a very great while, for the resemblance to boat timbers could scarcely be traced.

"Well, Jupiter picked up the parchment, wrapped the beetle in it, and gave it to me. Soon afterward we turned to go home and on the way met Lieutenant G——. I showed him the insect, and he begged me to let him take it to the fort. Upon my consenting, he thrust it forthwith into his waistcoat pocket, without the parchment in which it had been wrapped, which I had continued to hold in my hand during his inspection. Perhaps he dreaded my changing my mind and thought it best to make sure of the prize at once. You know how enthusiastic he is on all subjects connected with natural history. At the same time, without being conscious of it, I must have deposited the parchment in my own pocket.

"You remember that when I went to the table, for the purpose of making a sketch of the beetle, I found no paper where it was usually kept. I looked in the drawer and found none there. I searched my pockets, hoping to find an old letter, when my hand fell upon the parchment. I thus detail the precise mode in which it came into my possession, for the circumstances impressed me with peculiar force.

"No doubt you will think me fanciful—but I had already established a kind of *connection.* I had put together two links of a great chain. There was a boat lying upon a seacoast, and not far from the boat was a parchment—*not a paper*—with a skull depicted upon it. You will, of course, ask, 'Where is the connection?' I reply that the skull, or death's-head, is the well-known emblem of the pirate. The flag depicting the death's-head is hoisted in all engagements.

"I have said that the scrap was parchment and not paper. Parchment is durable—almost imperishable. Matters of little moment are rarely consigned to parchment, since, for the mere ordinary purposes of drawing or writing, it is not nearly so well adapted as paper. This reflection suggested some meaning—some relevancy—in the death's-head. I did not fail to observe, also, the *form* of the parchment. Although one of its corners had been, by some accident, destroyed, it could be seen that the original form was oblong. It was just such a slip, indeed, as might have been chosen for a memorandum—for a record of something to be long remembered and carefully preserved."

"But," I interposed, "you say that the skull was *not* upon the parchment when you made the drawing of the beetle. How, then, do you trace any connection between the boat and the skull, since this latter, according to your own admission, must have been designed (God only knows how or by whom) at some period subsequent to your sketching the scarabaeus?"

"Ah, hereupon turns the whole mystery, although the secret, at this point, I had comparatively little difficulty in solving. My steps were sure and could afford but a single result. I reasoned, for example, thus: When I drew the scarabaeus, there was no skull apparent upon the parchment. When I had completed the drawing, I gave it to you and observed you narrowly until you returned it. *You,* therefore, did not design the skull, and no one else was present to do it. Then it was not done by human agency. And nevertheless it was done.

"At this stage of my reflections, I endeavored to remember and *did* remember, with entire distinctness, every incident which occurred about the period in question. The weather was chilly (oh, rare and happy accident!), and a fire was blazing upon the hearth. I was heated with exercise and sat near the table. You, however, had drawn a chair close to the chimney. Just as I placed the parchment in your hand and as you were in the act of inspecting it, Wolf, the Newfoundland, entered and leaped upon your shoulders. With your left hand, you caressed him and kept him off, while your right, holding the parchment, was permitted to fall listlessly between your knees and in close proximity to the fire. At one moment I thought the blaze had caught it and was about to caution you, but before I could speak, you had withdrawn it and were engaged in its examination. When I considered all these particulars, I doubted not for a moment that *heat* had been the agent in bringing to light, upon the parchment, the skull which I saw designed upon it. You are well aware that chemical preparations exist, and have existed time out of mind, by means of which it is possible to write upon either paper or vellum so that the characters shall become visible only when subjected to the action of fire. Zaffer, digested in aqua regia and diluted with four times its weight of water, is sometimes employed; a green tint results. The regulus of cobalt, dissolved in spirit of niter, gives a red tint. These colors disappear at longer or shorter intervals after the material written upon cools, but again become apparent upon the reapplication of heat.

"I now scrutinized the death's-head with care. Its outer edges—the edges of the drawing nearest the edge of the vellum—were far more *distinct* than the others. It was clear that the action of the caloric had been imperfect or unequal. I immediately kindled a fire and subjected every portion of the parchment to a glowing heat. At first the only effect was the strengthening of the faint lines in the skull, but, upon persevering in the experiment, there became visible at the corner of the slip, diagonally opposite to the spot in which the death's-head was delineated, the figure of what I at first supposed to be a goat. A closer scrutiny, however, satisfied me that it was intended for a kid."

"Ha! Ha!" said I. "To be sure, I have no right to laugh at you—a million and a half of money is too serious a matter for mirth—but you are not about to establish a third link in your chain—you will not find any especial connection between your pirates and a goat. Pirates, you know, have nothing to do with goats; they appertain to the farming interest."

"But I have said that the figure was *not* that of a goat."

"Well, a kid, then—pretty much the same thing."

"Pretty much, but not altogether," said Legrand. "You may have heard of one *Captain* Kidd. I at once looked upon the figure of the animal as a kind of punning or hieroglyphical signature. I say signature, because its position upon the vellum suggested this idea. The death's-head at the corner diagonally opposite had, in the same manner, the air of a stamp, or seal. But I was sorely put out by the absence of all else—of the body to my imagined instrument—of the text for my context."

"I presume you expected to find a letter between the stamp and the signature."

"Something of that kind. The fact is, I felt irresistibly impressed with a presentiment of some vast good fortune impending. I can scarcely say why. Perhaps, after all, it was rather a desire than an actual belief; but do you know that Jupiter's silly words about the bug being of solid gold had a remarkable effect upon my fancy? And then the series of accidents and coincidences—these were so *very* extraordinary. Do you observe how mere an accident it was that these events should have occurred upon the *sole* day of all the year in which it has been, or may be, sufficiently cool for fire, and that without the fire or without the intervention of the dog at the precise moment in which he appeared, I should never have become aware of the death's-head and so never the possessor of the treasure?"

"But proceed—I am all impatience."

"Well, you have heard, of course, the many stories current—the thousand vague rumors afloat about money buried somewhere upon the Atlantic coast by Kidd and his associates. These rumors must have had some foundation in fact. And that the rumors have existed so long and so continuously could have resulted, it appeared to me, only from the circumstance of the buried treasure still *remaining* entombed. Had Kidd concealed his plunder for a time and afterward reclaimed it, the rumors would scarcely have reached us in their present unvarying form. You will observe that the stories told are all about money-seekers, not about money-finders. Had Kidd recovered his treasure, there the affair would have dropped. It seemed to me that some accident—say, the loss of a memorandum indicating its locality—had deprived him of the means of recovering it, and that this accident had become known to his followers, who otherwise might never have heard that treasure had been concealed at all and who, busying themselves in vain, because unguided, attempts to regain it, had given first birth, and then universal currency, to the reports which are now so common. Have you ever heard of any important treasure being unearthed along the coast?"

"Never."

"But that Kidd's accumulations were immense is well known. I took it for granted, therefore, that the earth still held them. You will scarcely be surprised when I tell you that I felt a hope, nearly amounting to certainty, that the parchment so strangely found involved a lost record of the place of deposit."

"But how did you proceed?"

"I held the vellum again to the fire, after increasing the heat, but nothing appeared. I now thought it possible that the coating of dirt might have something to do with the failure, so I carefully rinsed the parchment by pouring warm water over it, and, having done so, I placed it in a tin pan, with the skull downward, and put the pan upon a furnace of lighted charcoal. In a few minutes, the pan having become thoroughly heated, I removed the slip and, to my inexpressible joy, found it spotted in several places with what appeared to be figures arranged in lines. Again I placed it in the pan and suffered it to remain another minute. Upon taking it off, the whole was just as you see it now."

Here Legrand, having reheated the parchment, submitted it to my inspection. The following characters were rudely traced, in a red tint, between the death's-head and the goat:

53‡‡†305))6*;4826)4‡.)4‡);806*;48†8¶60))85;1‡(;:‡*8†8
3(88)5*†;46(;88*96*?;8)*‡(;485);5*†2:*‡(;4956*2(5*—4
)8¶8*;4069285);)6†8)4‡‡;1(‡9;48081;8:8‡1;48†85;4)485†5
28806*81(‡9;48;(88;4(‡?34;48)4‡;161;:188;‡?;

"But," said I, returning him the slip, "I am as much in the dark as ever. Were all the jewels of Golconda awaiting me upon my solution of this enigma, I am quite sure that I should be unable to earn them."

"And yet," said Legrand, "the solution is by no means so difficult as you might be led to imagine from the hasty inspection of the characters. These characters, as anyone might readily guess, form a cipher—that is to say, they convey a meaning. But, then, from what is known of Kidd, I could not suppose him capable of constructing any of the more abstruse cryptographs. I made up my mind at once that this was of a simple species—such, however, as would appear, to the crude intellect of the sailor, absolutely insoluble without the key."

"And you really solved it?"

"Readily. I have solved others of an abstruseness ten thousand times greater. Circumstances and a certain bias of mind have led me to take interest in such riddles, and it may well be doubted whether human ingenuity can construct an enigma of the kind which human ingenuity may not, by proper application, resolve. In fact, having once established connected and legible characters, I scarcely gave a thought to the mere discovery of their import.

"In the present case—indeed in all cases of secret writing—the first question regards the *language* of the cipher, for the principles of solution—so far, especially, as the more simple ciphers are concerned—depend upon and are varied by the genius of the particular idiom. In general, there is no alternative but experiment (directed by probabilities) of every tongue known to him who attempts the solution, until the true one be attained. But, with the cipher now before us, all difficulty was removed by the signature. The pun upon the word 'Kidd' is appreciable in no language other than the English. But for this consideration, I should have begun my attempts with the Spanish and French, as the tongues in which a secret of this kind would most naturally have been written by a pirate of the Spanish Main. As it was, I assumed the cryptograph to be English.

"You observe there are no divisions between the words. Had there been divisions, the task would have been comparatively easy. In such case I should have commenced with a collation and analysis of the shorter words, and had a word of a single letter occurred, as is most likely (*a* or *I*, for example), I should have considered the solution as assured. But, there being no division, my first step was to ascertain the predominant letters, as well as the least frequent. Counting all, I constructed a table thus:

Of the character 8	there are	33.
;	"	26.
4	"	19.
‡)	"	16.
*	"	13.
5	"	12.
6	"	11.
†1	"	8.
0	"	6.
92	"	5.
:3	"	4.
?	"	3.
¶	"	2.
—.	"	1.

"Now, in English the letter which most frequently occurs is *e*. Afterward, the succession runs thus: *a o i d h n r s t u y c f g l m w b k p q x z*. *E* predominates so remarkably that an individual sentence of any length is rarely seen in which it is not the prevailing character.

"Here, then, we have, in the very beginning, the groundwork for something more than a mere guess. The general use which may be made of the table is obvious—but in this particular cipher we shall only very partially require its aid. As our predominant character is 8, we will commence by assuming it as the *e* of the natural alphabet. To verify the supposition, let us observe if the 8 be seen often in couples—for *e* is doubled with great frequency in English, in such words, for example, as *meet, fleet, speed, seen, been, agree,* and so on. In the present instance, we see it doubled no less than five times.

"Let us assume 8, then, as *e*. Now, of all *words* in the language *the* is most usual; let us see, therefore, whether there are not repetitions of any three characters, in the same order of collocation, the last of them being 8. If we discover repetitions of such letters, so arranged, they will most probably represent the word *the*. Upon inspection, we find no less than seven such arrangements, the characters being ;48. We may, therefore, assume that ; represents *t*, 4 represents *h*, and 8 represents *e*—the last being now well confirmed. Thus a great step has been taken.

"But, having established a single word, we are enabled to establish a vastly important point—that is to say, several commencements and terminations of other words. Let us refer, for example, to the last instance but one, in which the combination ;48 occurs—not far from the end of the cipher. We know that the ; immediately ensuing is the commencement of a word, and of the six characters succeeding this *the*, we are cognizant of no less than five.

Let us set these characters down, thus, by the letters we know them to represent, leaving a space for the unknown:

t eeth.

"Here we are enabled at once to discard the *th,* as forming no portion of the word commencing with the first *t,* since, by experiment of the entire alphabet for a letter adapted to the vacancy, we perceive that no word can be formed of which this *th* can be a part. We are thus narrowed into

t ee,

and, going through the alphabet, if necessary, as before, we arrive at the word *tree* as the sole possible reading, with the exception of the rather unlikely *thee.* We thus gain another letter, *r,* represented by (, with the words *the tree* in juxtaposition.

"Looking beyond these words for a short distance, we again see the combination ;48 and employ it by way of *termination* to what immediately precedes. We have thus:

the tree ;4(‡?34 the,

or, substituting the natural letters, where known, it reads thus:

the tree thr‡?3h the.

"Now, if in place of the unknown characters, we leave blank spaces, or substitute dots, we read thus:

the tree thr...h the,

when the word *through* makes itself evident at once. But this discovery gives us three new letters, *o, u,* and *g,* represented by ‡, ?, and 3.

"Looking now, narrowly, through the cipher for combinations of known characters, we find, not very far from the beginning, this arrangement:

83(88, or egree,

which plainly is the conclusion of the word *degree* and gives us another letter, *d,* represented by †.

"Four letters beyond the word *degree,* we perceive the combinations

;46 (;88

"Translating the known characters and representing the unknown by dots, as before, we read thus:

th.rtee.,

an arrangement immediately suggestive of the word *thirteen* and again furnishing us with two new characters, *i* and *n,* represented by 6 and *.

"Referring now to the beginning of the cryptograph, we find the combination

53‡‡†.

"Translating as before, we obtain

.good,

which assures us that the first letter is *A* and that the first two words are *A good.*

"It is now time that we arrange our key, as far as discovered, in a tabular form, to avoid confusion. It will stand thus:

5	represents	a
†	"	d
8	"	e
3	"	g
4	"	h
6	"	i
*	"	n
‡	"	o
(	"	r
;	"	t

"We have, therefore, no fewer than ten of the most important letters represented, and it will be unnecessary to proceed with the details of the solution. I have said enough to convince you that ciphers of this nature are readily soluble and to give you some insight into the rationale of their development. But be assured that the specimen before us appertains to the very simplest species of cryptograph.

"It now only remains to give you the full translation of the characters upon the parchment as unriddled. Here it is:

> "A good glass in the bishop's hostel in the devil's seat forty-one degrees and thirteen minutes northeast and by north main branch seventh limb east side shoot from the left eye of the death's-head a beeline from the tree through the shot fifty feet out."

"But," said I, "the enigma seems still in as bad a condition as ever. How is it possible to extort a meaning from all this jargon about 'devil's seats,' 'death's-heads,' and 'bishop's hostels'?"

"I confess," replied Legrand, "that the matter still wears a serious aspect, when regarded with a casual glance. My first endeavor was to divide the sentence into the natural division intended by the cryptographist."

"You mean to punctuate it?"

"Something of that kind."

"But how was it possible to effect this?"

"I reflected that it had been a *point* with the writer to run his words together without division, so as to increase the difficulty of solution. Now, a not overacute man, in pursuing such an object, would be nearly certain to overdo the matter. When, in the course of his composition, he arrived at a break in his subject which would naturally require a pause or a point, he would be exceedingly apt to run his characters, at this place, more than usually close together. If you will observe the MS in the present instance, you will easily detect five such cases of unusual crowding. Acting upon this hint, I made the division into word groupings thus:

> "A good glass in the bishop's hostel in the devil's seat—forty-one degrees and thirteen minutes—northeast and by north—main branch seventh limb east side—shoot from the left eye of the death's-head—a beeline from the tree through the shot fifty feet out."

"Even this division," said I, "leaves me still in the dark."

"It left me also in the dark," replied Legrand, "for a few days, during which I made diligent inquiry, in the neighborhood of Sullivan's Island, for any building which went by the name of the 'Bishop's Hotel'; for, of course, I dropped the obsolete word 'hostel.' Gaining no information on the subject, I was on the point of extending my sphere of search and proceeding in a more systematic manner, when one morning it entered my head quite suddenly that this 'Bishop's Hostel' might have some reference to an old family, of the name of Bessop, which, time out of mind, had held possession of an ancient manor house about four miles to the northward of the island. I accordingly went over to the plantation and reinstituted my inquiries among the older Negroes of the place. At length one of the most aged of the women said that she had heard of such a place as *Bessop's Castle* and thought that she could guide me to it, but that it was not a castle nor a tavern but a high rock.

"I offered to pay her well for her trouble, and, after some demur, she consented to accompany me to the spot. We found it without much difficulty, and, dismissing her, I proceeded to examine the place. The 'castle' consisted of an irregular assemblage of cliffs and rocks, one of the latter being quite remarkable for its height as well as for its insulated and artificial appearance. I clambered to its apex and then felt much at a loss as to what should be done next.

"While I was busied in reflection, my eyes fell upon a narrow ledge in the eastern face of the rock, perhaps a yard below the summit upon which I stood. This ledge projected about eighteen inches and was not more than a foot wide, while a niche in the cliff just above it gave it a rude resemblance to one of the hollow-backed chairs used by our ancestors. I made no doubt that here was the 'devil's seat' alluded to in the MS, and now I seemed to grasp the full secret of the riddle.

"The 'good glass,' I knew, could have reference to nothing but a telescope, for the word 'glass' is rarely employed in any other sense by seamen. Now, here, I at once saw, was a telescope to be used and a definite point of view, *admitting no variation,* from which to use it. Nor did I hesitate to believe that the phrases, 'forty-one degrees and thirteen minutes' and 'northeast and by north' were intended as directions for the leveling of the glass. Greatly excited by these discoveries, I hurried home, procured a telescope, and returned to the rock.

"I let myself down to the ledge and found that it was impossible to retain a seat upon it except in one particular position. This fact confirmed my preconceived idea. I proceeded to use the glass.

"Of course, the 'forty-one degrees and thirteen minutes' could allude to nothing but elevation above the visible horizon, since the horizontal direction was clearly indicated by the words, 'northeast and by north.' This latter direction I at once established by means of a pocket compass; then, pointing the glass as nearly at an angle of forty-one degrees of elevation as I could do it by guess, I moved it cautiously up or down, until my attention was arrested by a circular rift or opening in the foliage of a large tree that overtopped its fellows in the distance. In the center of this rift, I perceived a white spot but could not at first distinguish what it was. Adjusting the focus of the telescope, I again looked and now made it out to be a human skull.

"Upon this discovery, I was so sanguine as to consider the enigma solved; for the phrase 'main branch, seventh limb, east side' could refer only to the position of the skull upon the tree, while 'shoot from the left eye of the death's-head' admitted also of but one interpretation, in regard to a search for buried treasure. I perceived that the design was to drop a bullet from the left eye of the skull and that a beeline, or, in other words, a straight line, drawn from the nearest point of the trunk through 'the shot' (or the spot where the bullet fell) and thence extended to a distance of fifty feet would indicate a definite point—and beneath this point I thought it at least *possible* that a deposit of value lay concealed."

"All this," I said, "is exceedingly clear and, although ingenious, still simple and explicit. When you left the 'Bishop's Hostel,' what then?"

"Why, having carefully taken the bearings of the tree, I turned homeward. The instant that I left the 'devil's seat,' however, the circular rift vanished. Nor could I get a glimpse of it afterward, turn as I would. What seems to me the chief ingenuity in this whole business is the fact (for repeated experiment has convinced me it *is* a fact) that the circular opening in question is visible from no other attainable point of view than that afforded by the narrow ledge upon the face of the rock.

"In this expedition to the 'Bishop's Hostel,' I had been attended by Jupiter, who had no doubt observed for some weeks past the abstraction of my demeanor and took especial care not to leave me alone. But, on the next day, getting up very early, I contrived to give him the slip and went into the hills in search of the tree. After much toil, I found it. When I came home at night my valet proposed to give me a flogging. With the rest of the adventure, I believe you are as well acquainted as I."

"I suppose," said I, "you missed the spot, in the first attempt at digging, through Jupiter's stupidity in letting the bug fall through the right instead of the left eye of the skull."

"Precisely. This mistake made a difference of about two inches and a half in the 'shot'—that is to say, in the position of the peg nearest the tree—and had the treasure been *beneath* the 'shot,' the error would have been of little moment; but the 'shot,' together with the nearest point of the tree, were merely two points for the establishment of a line of direction; of course, the error, however trivial in the beginning, increased as we proceeded with the line, and by the time we had gone fifty feet, this threw us quite off the scent. But for my deep-seated impressions that treasure was here somewhere actually buried, we might have had all our labor in vain."

"But your grandiloquence and your conduct in swinging the beetle—how excessively odd! I was sure you were mad. And why did you insist upon letting fall the bug, instead of a bullet, from the skull?"

"Why, to be frank, I felt somewhat annoyed by your evident suspicions touching my sanity and so resolved to punish you quietly, in my own way, by a little bit of sober mystification. For this reason I swung the beetle, and for this reason I let it fall from the tree. An observation of yours about its great weight suggested the latter idea."

"Yes, I perceive. And now there is only one point which puzzles me. What are we to make of the skeletons found in the hole?"

"That is a question I am no more able to answer than you. There seems, however, only one plausible way of accounting for them—and yet it is dreadful to believe in such atrocity as my suggestion would imply. It is clear that Kidd—if Kidd indeed secreted this treasure, which I doubt not—it is clear that he must have had assistance in the labor. But this labor concluded, he may have thought it expedient to remove all participants in his secret. Perhaps a couple of blows with a mattock were sufficient, while his coadjutors were busy in the pit; perhaps it required a dozen—who shall tell?"

A Descent into the Maelström

WE HAD NOW REACHED the summit of the loftiest crag. For some minutes the old man seemed too much exhausted to speak.

"Not long ago," said he at length, "and I could have guided you on this route as well as the youngest of my sons, but about three years past, there happened to me an event such as never happened before to mortal man—or at least such as no man ever survived to tell of—and the six hours of deadly terror which I then endured have broken me up, body and soul. You suppose me a *very* old man—but I am not. It took less than a single day to change these hairs from a jetty black to white, to weaken my limbs, and to unstring my nerves so that I tremble at the least exertion and am frightened at a shadow. Do you know I can scarcely look over this little cliff without getting giddy?"

The "little cliff"—upon whose edge he had so carelessly thrown himself down that the weightier portion of his body hung over it, while he was only kept from falling by the tenure of his elbow on its extreme and slippery edge—this "little cliff" arose, a sheer, unobstructed precipice of black, shining rock, some fifteen or sixteen hundred feet from the world of crags beneath us. Nothing would have tempted me to within half a dozen yards of its brink. In truth, so deeply was I excited by the perilous position of my companion that I fell at full length upon the ground, clung to the shrubs around me, and dared not even glance upward at the sky—while I struggled in vain to divest myself of the idea that the very foundations of the mountain were in danger from the fury of the winds. It was long before I could reason myself into sufficient courage to sit up and look out into the distance.

"You must get over these fancies," said the guide, "for I have brought you here that you might have the best possible view of the scene of that event I mentioned—and to tell you the whole story, with the spot just under your eye.

"We are now—" he continued in that particularizing manner which distinguished him, "we are now close upon the Norwegian coast—in the sixty-eighth degree of latitude, in the great province of Nordland, and in the dreary district of Lofoden. The mountain upon whose top we sit is Helseggen, the Cloudy. Now raise yourself up a little higher—hold on to the grass if you feel giddy—so—and look out, beyond the belt of vapor beneath us, into the sea."

I looked dizzily and beheld a wide expanse of ocean whose waters wore so inky a hue as to bring at once to my mind the Nubian geographer's account of the *Mare Tenebrarum*. A panorama more deplorably desolate no human imagination can conceive. To the right and left, as far as the eye could reach, there lay outstretched, like ramparts of the world, lines of horridly black and beetling cliff, whose character of gloom was but the more forcibly illustrated by the surf, which reared high up against it, its white and ghastly crest howling and shrieking forever. Just opposite the promontory upon whose apex we were placed and at a distance of some five or six miles out at sea, there was visible a small, bleak-looking island; or, more properly, its position was discernible through the wilderness of surge in which it was enveloped. About two miles nearer the land arose another of smaller size, hideously craggy and barren, encompassed at various intervals by clusters of dark rocks.

The appearance of the ocean, in the space between the more distant island and the shore, had something very unusual about it. Although, at the time, so strong a gale was blowing landward that a brig in the remote offing lay to under a double-reefed trysail and constantly plunged her whole hull out of sight, still there was here nothing like a regular swell but only a short, quick, angry cross-dashing of water in every direction—as well in the teeth of the wind as otherwise. Of foam there was little, except in the immediate vicinity of the rocks.

"The island in the distance," resumed the old man, "is called by the Norwegians Vurrgh. The one midway is Moskoe. That a mile to the northward is Ambaaren. Yonder are Islesen, Hotholm, Keildhelm, Suarven, and Buckholm. Farther off—between Moskoe and Vurrgh—are Otterholm, Flimen, Sandflesen, and Stockholm. These are the true names of the places—but why it has been thought necessary to name them at all is more than either you or I can understand. Do you hear anything? Do you see any change in the water?"

We had now been about ten minutes upon the top of Helseggen, to which we had ascended from the interior of Lofoden, so that we had caught no glimpse of the sea until it had burst upon us as we achieved the summit. As the old man spoke, I became aware of a loud and gradually increasing sound, like the moaning of a vast herd of buffalo upon an American prairie, and at the same moment I perceived that what seamen term the *chopping* character of the ocean beneath us was rapidly changing into a current which set to the eastward. Even while I

gazed, this current acquired a monstrous velocity. Each moment added to its speed—to its headlong impetuosity. In five minutes the whole sea as far as Vurrgh was lashed into ungovernable fury. But it was between Moskoe and the coast that the main uproar held its sway. Here the vast bed of the waters, seamed and scarred into a thousand conflicting channels, burst suddenly into frenzied convulsion—heaving, boiling, hissing, gyrating in gigantic and innumerable vortices, and all whirling and plunging on to the eastward with a rapidity which water never elsewhere assumes except in precipitous descents.

In a few minutes more, there came over the scene another radical alteration. The general surface grew somewhat more smooth, and the whirlpools one by one disappeared, while prodigious streaks of foam became apparent where none had been seen before. These streaks, at length, spreading out to a great distance and entering into combination, took unto themselves the gyratory motion of the subsided vortices and seemed to form the germ of another more vast. Suddenly—very suddenly—this assumed a distinct and definite existence in a circle of more than a mile in diameter. The edge of the whirl was represented by a broad belt of gleaming spray; but no particle of this slipped into the mouth of the terrific funnel, whose interior, as far as the eye could fathom it, was a smooth, shining, jet black wall of water, inclined to the horizon at an angle of some forty-five degrees, speeding dizzily round and round with a swaying and sweltering motion and sending forth to the winds an appalling voice, half shriek, half roar, such as not even the mighty cataract of Niagara ever lifts up, in its agony, to heaven.

The mountain trembled to its very base, and the rock rocked. I threw myself upon my face and clung to the scant herbage in an excess of nervous agitation.

"This—" said I at length to the old man, "this *can* be nothing else than the great whirlpool of the Maelström."

"So it is sometimes termed," said he. "We Norwegians call it the Moskoe-ström, from the island of Moskoe in the midway."

The ordinary accounts of this vortex had by no means prepared me for what I saw. That of Jonas Ramus, which is perhaps the most circumstantial of any, cannot impart the faintest conception of either the magnificence or the horror of the scene—or of the wild, bewildering sense of the *novel* which confounds the beholder. I am not sure from what point of view the writer in question surveyed it nor at what time, but it could have been neither from the summit of Helseggen nor during a storm. There are some passages of his description, nevertheless, which may be quoted for their details, although their effect is exceedingly feeble in conveying an impression of the spectacle.

"Between Lofoden and Moskoe," he says, "the depth of the water is between thirty-five and forty fathoms; but on the other side, toward Ver (Vurrgh), this depth decreases so as not to afford a convenient passage for a vessel without the risk of splitting on the rocks, which happens even in the calmest weather. When it is flood, the stream runs up the country between Lofoden and Moskoe with a boisterous rapidity, but the roar of its impetuous ebb to the sea is scarce equaled by the loudest and most dreadful cataracts—the noise being heard several leagues off—and the vortices or pits are of such an extent and depth that if a ship comes within its attraction, it is inevitably absorbed and carried down to the bottom and there beat to pieces against the rocks, and when the water relaxes, the fragments thereof are thrown up again. But these intervals of tranquillity are only at the turn of the ebb and flood, in calm weather, and last but a quarter of an hour, its violence gradually returning. When the stream is most boisterous and its fury heightened by a storm, it is dangerous to come within a Norway mile of it. Boats, yachts, and ships have been carried away by not guarding against it before they were within its reach. It likewise happens frequently that whales come too near the stream and are overpowered by its violence, and then it is impossible to describe their howlings and bellowings in their fruitless struggles to disengage themselves. Once, a bear, attempting to swim from Lofoden to Moskoe, was caught by the stream and borne down, while he roared terribly, so as to be heard on shore. Large stocks of firs and pine trees, after being absorbed by the current, rise again broken and torn to such a degree as if bristles grew upon them. This plainly shows the bottom to consist of craggy rocks, among which they are whirled to and fro. This stream is regulated by the flux and reflux of the sea —it being constantly high and low water every six hours. In the year 1645, early in the morning of Sexagesima Sunday, it raged with such noise and impetuosity that the very stones of the houses on the coast fell to the ground."

In regard to the depth of the water, I could not see how this could have been ascertained at all in the immediate vicinity of the vortex. The "forty fathoms" must have reference only to portions of the channel close upon the shore either of Moskoe or Lofoden. The depth in the center of the Moskoe-ström must be immeasurably greater, and no better proof of this fact is necessary than can be obtained from even the sidelong glance into the abyss of the whirl, which may be had from the highest crag of Helseggen. Looking down from this pinnacle upon the howling Phlegethon below, I could not help smiling at the simplicity with which the honest Jonas Ramus records, as a matter difficult of belief, the anecdotes of the whales and the bears, for it appeared to me, in fact, a self-evident thing that the largest ship of the line in existence, coming within the influence of that deadly attraction, could resist it as little as a feather the hurricane and must disappear bodily and at once.

The attempts to account for the phenomenon—some of which, I remember, seemed to me sufficiently plausible in perusal—now wore a very different and unsatisfactory aspect. The idea generally received is that this, as well as three smaller vortices among the Ferroe Islands, has "no other cause than the collision of waves rising and falling at flux and reflux against a ridge of rocks and shelves, which confines the water, so that it precipitates itself like a cataract; and thus the higher the flood rises, the deeper must the fall be, and the natural result of all is as a whirlpool or vortex, the prodigious suction of which is sufficiently known by lesser experiments." These are the words of the *Encyclopaedia Britannica.* Kircher and others imagine that in the center of the channel of the Maelström is an abyss penetrating the globe and issuing in some very remote part—the Gulf of Bothnia being somewhat decidedly named in one instance. This opinion, idle in itself, was the one to which, as I gazed, my imagination most readily assented; and, mentioning it to the guide, I was rather surprised to hear him say that, although it was the view of the subject almost universally held by the Norwegians, it nevertheless was not his own. As to the former notion, he confessed his inability to comprehend it, and here I agreed with him—for, however conclusive on paper, it becomes altogether unintelligible, even absurd, amid the thunder of the abyss.

"You have had a good look at the whirl now," said the old man, "and if you will creep round this crag, so as to get in its lee and deaden the roar of the water, I will tell you a story that will convince you I ought to know something of the Moskoe-ström."

I placed myself as desired, and he proceeded.

"Myself and my two brothers once owned a schooner-rigged smack of about seventy tons' burden, with which we were in the habit of fishing among the islands beyond Moskoe, nearly to Vurrgh. In all violent eddies at sea, there is good fishing at proper opportunities if one has only the courage to attempt it, but among the whole of the Lofoden coast men, we three were the only ones who made a regular business of going out to the islands, as I tell you. The usual grounds are a great way lower down to the southward. There fish can be gotten at all hours without much risk, and therefore these places are preferred. The choice spots over here among the rocks, however, not only yield the finest variety but in far greater abundance, so that we often got in a single day what the more timid of the craft could not scrape together in a week. In fact, we made it a matter of desperate speculation—the risk of life standing instead of labor, and courage answering for capital.

"We kept the smack in a cove about five miles higher up the coast than this, and it was our practice, in fine weather, to take advantage of the fifteen minutes' slack to push across the main channel of the Moskoe-ström, far above the pool, and then drop down upon anchorage somewhere near Otterholm or Sandflesen, where the eddies are not so violent as elsewhere. Here we used to remain until nearly time for slack water again, when we weighed and made for home. We never set out upon this expedition without a steady side wind for going and coming—one that we felt sure would not fail us before our return—and we seldom made a miscalculation upon this point. Twice during six years we were forced to stay all night at anchor on account of a dead calm, which is a rare thing indeed just about here; and once we had to remain on the grounds nearly a week, nearly starving to death, owing to a gale which blew up shortly after our arrival and made the channel too boisterous to be thought of. Upon this occasion, we should have been driven out to sea, in spite of everything (for the whirlpools threw us round and round so violently that at length we fouled our anchor and dragged it), if it had not been that we drifted into one of the innumerable crosscurrents—here today and gone tomorrow—which drove us under the lee of Flimen, where, by good luck, we brought up.

"I could not tell you the twentieth part of the difficulties we encountered on the grounds—it is a bad spot to be in, even in good weather—but we made shift always to run the gauntlet of the Moskoe-ström itself without accident, although at times my heart has been in my mouth when we happened to be a minute or so behind or before the slack. The wind sometimes was not as strong as we thought it at starting, and then we made rather less way than we could wish, while the current rendered the smack unmanageable. My eldest brother had a son eighteen years old, and I had two stout boys of my own. These would have been of great assistance at such times in using the sweeps, as well as afterward in fishing, but somehow, although we ran the risk ourselves, we had not the heart to let the young ones get into the danger—for, after all is said and done, it *was* a horrible danger, and that is the truth.

"It is now within a few days of three years since what I am going to tell you occurred. It was on the tenth day of July, 18—, a day which the people of this part of the world will never forget—for it was one in which blew the most terrible hurricane that ever came out of the heavens;

and yet all the morning and, indeed, until late in the afternoon, there was a gentle and steady breeze from the southwest, while the sun shone brightly, so that the oldest seaman among us could not have foreseen what was to follow.

"The three of us—my two brothers and myself—had crossed over to the islands about two P.M. and had soon nearly loaded the smack with fine fish, which, we all remarked, were more plentiful that day than we had ever known them to be. It was just seven *by my watch* when we weighed and started for home, so as to make the worst of the Ström at slack water, which we knew would be at eight.

"We set out with a fresh wind on our starboard quarter and for some time spanked along at a great rate, never dreaming of danger, for indeed we saw not the slightest reason to apprehend it. All at once we were taken aback by a breeze from over Helseggen. This was most unusual —something that had never happened to us before—and I began to feel a little uneasy, without exactly knowing why. We put the boat on the wind but could make no headway at all for the eddies, and I was just upon the point of proposing to return to the anchorage, when, looking astern, we saw the whole horizon covered with a singular copper-colored cloud that rose with the most amazing velocity.

"In the meantime the breeze that had headed us off fell away, and we were dead becalmed, drifting about in every direction. This state of things, however, did not last long enough to give us time to think about it. In less than a minute, the storm was upon us—in less than two, the sky was entirely overcast—and, what with this and the driving spray, it became suddenly so dark that we could not see each other in the smack.

"Such a hurricane as then blew, it is folly to attempt describing. The oldest seaman in Norway never experienced anything like it. We had let our sails go by the run before it cleverly took us, but at the first puff, both our masts went by the board, as if they had been sawed off—the mainmast taking with it my youngest brother, who had lashed himself to it for safety.

"Our boat was the lightest feather of a thing that ever sat upon water. It had a complete flush deck, with only a small hatch near the bow, and this hatch it had always been our custom to batten down when about to cross the Ström, by way of precaution against the chopping seas. But for this circumstance, we should have foundered at once—for we lay entirely buried for some moments. How my elder brother escaped destruction I cannot say, for I never had an opportunity of ascertaining. For my part, as soon as I had let the foresail run, I threw myself flat on the deck, with my feet against the narrow gunwhale of the bow and with my hands grasping a ringbolt near the foot of the foremast. It was mere instinct that prompted me to do this—which was undoubtedly the very best thing I could have done—for I was too much flurried to think.

"For some moments we were completely deluged, as I say, and all this time I held my breath and clung to the bolt. When I could stand it no longer, I raised myself up on my knees, still keeping hold with my hands, and got my head clear. Presently our little boat gave herself a shake, just as a dog does in coming out of the water, and thus rid herself in some measure of the seas. I was now trying to get the better of the stupor that had come over me and to collect my senses, so as to see what was to be done, when I felt somebody grasp my arm. It was my elder brother, and my heart leaped for joy, for I was sure that he had gone overboard—but the next moment all this joy was turned into horror, for he put his mouth close to my ear and screamed out the word *'Moskoe-ström!'*

"No one ever will know what my feelings were at that moment. I shook from head to foot, as if I had had the most violent fit of the ague. I knew what he meant by that one word well enough—I knew what he wished to make me understand. With the wind that now drove us on, we were bound for the whirl of the Ström, and nothing could save us!

"You perceive that, in crossing the Ström *channel,* we always went a long way up above the whirl, even in the calmest weather, and then had to wait and watch carefully for the slack—but now we were driving right upon the pool itself, and in such a hurricane as this! *To be sure,* I thought, *we shall get there just about the slack—there is some little hope in that*—but in the next moment I cursed myself for being so great a fool as to dream of hope at all. I knew very well that we were doomed had we been ten times a ninety-gun ship.

"By this time, the first fury of the tempest had spent itself, or perhaps we did not feel it so much as we scudded before it, but, at all events, the seas, which at first had been kept down by the wind and lay flat and frothing, now got up into absolute mountains. A singular change, too, had come over the heavens. Around in every direction, it was still as black as pitch, but nearly overhead there burst out all at once a circular rift of clear sky—as clear as I ever saw, and of a deep, bright blue—and through it there blazed forth the full moon, with a luster that I never before knew her to wear. She lit up everything about us with the greatest distinctness—but O God, what a scene it was to light up!

"I now made one or two attempts to speak to my brother—but, in some manner which I could not understand, the din had so increased that I could not make him hear a single word, although I screamed at the top of my voice in his ear. Presently he shook his head, looking as pale as death, and held up one of his fingers, as if to say, '*Listen!*'

"At first I could not make out what he meant, but soon a hideous thought flashed upon me. I dragged my watch from its fob. It was not going. I glanced at its face by the moonlight, and then burst into tears as I flung it far away into the ocean. *It had run down at seven o'clock! We were behind the time of the slack, and the whirl of the Ström was in full fury!*

"When a boat is well built, properly trimmed, and not deeply laden, the waves in a strong gale, when she is going large, seem always to slip from beneath her—which appears very strange to a landsman—and this is what is called *riding,* in sea phrase. Well, so far, we had ridden the swells very cleverly, but presently a gigantic sea happened to take us right under the counter, and it bore us with it as it rose—up—up—as if into the sky. I would not have believed that any wave could rise so high. And then down we came with a sweep, a slide, and a plunge that made me feel sick and dizzy, as if I was falling from some lofty mountaintop in a dream. But while we were up, I had thrown a quick glance around—and that one glance was all-sufficient. I saw our exact position in an instant. The Moskoe-ström whirlpool was about a quarter of a mile dead ahead, but no more like the everyday Moskoe-ström than the whirl, as you now see it, is like a millrace. If I had not known where we were and what we had to expect, I should not have recognized the place at all. As it was, I involuntarily closed my eyes in horror. The lids clenched themselves together, as if in a spasm.

"It could not have been more than two minutes afterward until we suddenly felt the waves subside, and we were enveloped in foam. The boat made a sharp half-turn to larboard and then shot off in its new direction like a thunderbolt. At the same moment, the roaring noise of the water was completely drowned in a kind of shrill shriek —such a sound as you might imagine given out by the waste pipes of many thousand steam vessels letting off their steam all together. We were now in the belt of surf which always surrounds the whirl, and I thought, of course, that another moment would plunge us into the abyss—down which we could see only indistinctly, on account of the amazing velocity with which we were borne along. The boat did not seem to sink into the water at all but to skim like an air bubble upon the surface of the surge. Her starboard side was next the whirl, and on the larboard arose the world of ocean we had left. It stood like a huge writhing wall between us and the horizon.

"It may appear strange, but now, when we were in the very jaws of the gulf, I felt more composed than when we were only approaching it. Having made up my mind to hope no more, I got rid of a great deal of that terror which unmanned me at first. I suppose it was despair that strung my nerves.

"It may look like boasting, but what I tell you is truth: I began to reflect how magnificent a thing it was to die in such a manner and how foolish it was of me to think of so paltry a consideration as my own individual life, in view of so wonderful a manifestation of God's power. I do believe that I blushed with shame when this idea crossed my mind. After a little while I became possessed with the keenest curiosity about the whirl itself. I positively felt a *wish* to explore its depths, even at the sacrifice I was going to make, and my principal grief was that I should never be able to tell my old companions on shore about the mysteries I should see. These, no doubt, were singular fancies to occupy a man's mind in such extremity, and I have often thought since that the revolution of the boat around the pool might have rendered me a little light-headed.

"There was another circumstance which tended to restore my self-possession, and this was the cessation of the wind, which could not reach us in our present situation—for, as you saw yourself, the belt of surf is considerably lower than the general bed of the ocean, and this latter now towered above us, a high, black mountainous ridge. If you have never been at sea in a heavy gale, you can form no idea of the confusion of mind occasioned by the wind and spray together. They blind, deafen, and strangle you, and take away all power of action or reflection. But we were now, in a great measure, rid of these annoyances—just as death-condemned felons in prison are allowed petty indulgences forbidden them while their doom is yet uncertain.

"How often we made the circuit of the belt it is impossible to say. We careered round and round for perhaps an hour, flying rather than floating, getting gradually more and more into the middle of the surge and then nearer and nearer to its horrible inner edge. All this time I had never let go of the ringbolt. My brother was at the stern, holding on to a small empty water cask which had been securely lashed under the coop of the counter and was the only thing on deck that had not been swept overboard when the gale first took us. As we approached the brink of the pit, he let go his hold upon this and made for the ring, from which, in the agony of his terror, he endeavored to force my hands, as it was not large enough to afford us both a secure grasp. I never felt deeper grief than when

I saw him attempt this act, although I knew he was a madman when he did it—a raving maniac, through sheer fright. I did not care, however, to contest the point with him. I knew it could make no difference whether either of us held on at all, so I let him have the bolt and went astern to the cask. This there was no great difficulty in doing, for the smack flew round steadily enough and upon an even keel, only swaying to and fro with the immense sweeps and swelters of the whirl. Scarcely had I secured myself in my new position, when we gave a wild lurch to starboard and rushed headlong into the abyss. I muttered a hurried prayer to God and thought all was over.

"As I felt the sickening sweep of the descent, I had instinctively tightened my hold upon the barrel and closed my eyes. For some seconds I dared not open them, while I expected instant destruction and wondered that I was not already in my death struggles with the water. But moment after moment elapsed. I still lived. The sense of falling had ceased, and the motion of the vessel seemed much as it had been before, while in the belt of foam, with the exception that she now lay more along. I took courage and looked once again upon the scene.

"Never shall I forget the sensations of awe, horror, and admiration with which I gazed about me. The boat appeared to be hanging, as if by magic, midway down, upon the interior surface of a funnel vast in circumference and prodigious in depth, whose perfectly smooth sides might have been mistaken for ebony but for the bewildering rapidity with which they spun around and the gleaming and ghastly radiance they shot forth as the rays of the full moon, from that circular rift amid the clouds which I have already described, streamed in a flood of golden glory along the black walls and far away down into the inmost recesses of the abyss.

"At first I was too much confused to observe anything accurately. The general burst of terrific grandeur was all that I beheld. When I recovered myself a little, however, my gaze fell instinctively downward. In this direction, I was able to obtain an unobstructed view from the manner in which the smack hung on the inclined surface of the pool. She was quite upon an even keel—that is to say, her deck lay in a plane parallel with that of the water, but this latter sloped at an angle of more than forty-five degrees, so that we seemed to be lying upon our beam-ends. I could not help observing, nevertheless, that I had scarcely more difficulty in maintaining my hold and footing in this situation than if we had been upon a dead level, and this, I suppose, was owing to the speed at which we revolved.

"The rays of the moon seemed to search the very bottom of the profound gulf, but still I could make out nothing distinctly, on account of a thick mist in which everything there was enveloped and over which there hung a magnificent rainbow, like that narrow and tottering bridge which Mussulmen say is the only pathway between Time and Eternity. This mist, or spray, was no doubt occasioned by the clashing of the great walls of the funnel as they all met together at the bottom, but the yell that went up to the heavens from out of that mist I dare not attempt to describe.

"Our first slide into the abyss itself, from the belt of foam above, had carried us a great distance down the slope, but our further descent was by no means proportionate. Round and round we swept, not with any uniform movement but in dizzying swings and jerks that sent us sometimes only a few hundred yards, sometimes nearly the complete circuit of the whirl. Our progress downward at each revolution was slow but very perceptible.

"Looking about me upon the wide waste of liquid ebony on which we were thus borne, I perceived that our boat was not the only object in the embrace of the whirl. Both above and below us were visible fragments of vessels, large masses of building timber, and trunks of trees, with many smaller articles, such as pieces of house furniture, broken boxes, barrels, and staves. I have already described the unnatural curiosity which had taken the place of my original terrors. It appeared to grow upon me as I drew nearer and nearer to my dreadful doom. I now began to watch, with a strange interest, the numerous things that floated in our company. I *must* have been delirious, for I even sought *amusement* in speculating upon the relative velocities of their several descents toward the foam below. 'This fir tree,' I found myself at one time saying, 'will certainly be the next thing that takes the awful plunge and disappears'—and then I was disappointed to find that the wreck of a Dutch merchant ship overtook it and went down before. At length, after making several guesses of this nature and being deceived in all, this fact—the fact of my invariable miscalculation—set me upon a train of reflection that made my limbs again tremble, and my heart beat heavily once more.

"It was not a new terror that thus affected me but the dawn of a more exciting *hope*. This hope arose partly from memory and partly from present observation. I called to mind the great variety of buoyant matter that strewed the coast of Lofoden, having been absorbed and then thrown forth by the Moskoe-ström. By far the greater number of the articles were shattered in the most extraordinary way—so chafed and roughened as to have the appearance of being stuck full of splinters—but then I distinctly recollected that there were *some* of them which were not disfigured at all. Now, I could not account for this difference except by supposing that the roughened fragments were the only ones which had been *completely absorbed,* and that the others had entered the whirl at so late a period of the tide or, for some reason, had descended so slowly after entering that they did not reach the bottom before the turn of the flood came, or of the ebb, as the case might be. I conceived it possible, in either instance, that they might thus be whirled up again to the level of the ocean, without undergoing the fate of those which had been drawn in earlier or absorbed more rapidly. I made also three important observations. The first was that, as a general rule, the larger the bodies were, the more rapid their descent; the second, that, between two masses of equal extent, the one spherical and the other *of any other shape,* the superiority in speed of descent was with the sphere; the third, that, between two masses of equal size, the one cylindrical and the other of any other shape, the cylinder was absorbed the more slowly. Since my escape, I have had several conversations on this subject with an old schoolmaster of the district, and it was from him that I learned the use of the words 'cylinder' and 'sphere.' He explained to me—although I have forgotten the explanation—how what I observed was, in fact, the natural consequence of the forms of the floating fragments and showed me how it happened that a cylinder swimming in a vortex offered more resistance to its suction and was drawn in with greater difficulty than an equally bulky body of any other form whatever.

"There was one startling circumstance which went a great way in enforcing these observations and rendering me anxious to turn them to account, and this was that at every revolution we passed something like a barrel, or else the yard or the mast of a vessel, while many of those things which had been on our level when I first opened my eyes upon the wonders of the whirlpool were now high up above us and seemed to have moved but little from their original station.

"I no longer hesitated in deciding what to do. I resolved to lash myself securely to the water cask on to which I now held, to cut it loose from the counter, and to throw myself with it into the water. I attracted my brother's attention by signs, pointed to the floating barrels that came near us, and did everything in my power to make him understand what I was about to do. I thought at length that he comprehended my design, but, whether this was the case or not, he shook his head despairingly and refused to move from his station by the ringbolt. It was impossible to reach him—the emergency admitted of no delay—and so, with a bitter struggle, I resigned him to his fate, fastened myself to the cask by means of the lashings which secured it to the counter, and precipitated myself with it into the sea without further hesitation.

"The result was precisely what I had hoped it might be. As it is I myself who now tell you this tale—as you see that I *did* escape—and as you are already in possession of the mode in which this escape was effected and must therefore anticipate all that I have further to say, I will bring my story quickly to conclusion. It might have been an hour or thereabouts after my quitting the smack, when, having descended to a vast distance beneath me, it made three or four wild gyrations in rapid succession and, bearing my loved brother with it, plunged headlong, at once and forever, into the chaos of foam below. The barrel to which I was attached sank very little farther than half the distance between the bottom of the gulf and the spot at which I leaped overboard, before a great change took place in the character of the whirlpool. The slope of the sides of the vast funnel became momently less and less steep. The gyrations of the whirl grew gradually less and less violent. By degrees, the froth and the rainbow disappeared, and the bottom of the gulf seemed slowly to uprise. The sky was clear, the winds had gone down, and the full moon was setting radiantly in the west when I found myself on the surface of the ocean, in full view of the shores of Lofoden and above the spot where the pool of the Moskoe-ström *had been*. It was the hour of the slack—but the sea still heaved in mountainous waves from the effects of the hurricane. I was borne violently into the channel of the Ström and in a few minutes was hurried down the coast into the grounds of the fishermen. A boat picked me up, exhausted from fatigue and (now that the danger was removed) speechless from the memory of its horror. Those who drew me on board were my old mates and daily companions, but they knew me no more than they would have known a traveler from the spirit land. My hair, which had been raven black the day before, was as white as you see it now. They say, too, that the whole expression of my countenance had changed. I told them my story—they did not believe it. I now tell it to *you,* and I can scarcely expect you to put more faith in it than did the merry fishermen of Lofoden."

William Wilson

LET ME CALL MYSELF, for the present, William Wilson. The fair page now lying before me need not be sullied with my real appellation. This has been already too much an object for the scorn, for the horror, for the detestation of my race. To the uttermost regions of the globe have not the indignant winds bruited its unparalleled infamy? O outcast of all outcasts most abandoned! To the earth are thou not forever dead? To its honors, to its flowers, to its golden aspirations? And a cloud, dense, dismal, and limitless, does it not hang eternally between thy hopes and heaven?

I would not, if I could, here or today, embody a record of my later years of unspeakable misery and unpardonable crime. This epoch—these later years—took unto itself a sudden elevation in turpitude, whose origin alone it is my present purpose to assign. Men usually grow base by degrees. From me, in an instant, all virtue dropped bodily, as a mantle. From comparatively trivial wickedness, I passed, with the stride of a giant, into more than the enormities of an Elagabalus. What chance—what one event—brought this evil thing to pass, bear with me while I relate. Death approaches, and the shadow which foreruns him has thrown a softening influence over my spirit. I long, in passing through the dim valley, for the sympathy—I had nearly said for the pity—of my fellowmen. I would fain have them believe that I have been, in some measure, the slave of circumstances beyond human control. I would wish them to seek out for me, in the details I am about to give, some little oasis of *fatality* amid a wilderness of error. I would have them allow what they cannot refrain from allowing: that, although temptation may have erewhile existed as great, man was never *thus*, at least, tempted before, certainly never *thus* fell. And is it, therefore, that he has never thus suffered? Have I not indeed been living in a dream? And am I not now dying a victim to the horror and the mystery of the wildest of all sublunary visions?

I am the descendant of a race whose imaginative and easily excitable temperament has at all times rendered them remarkable, and in my earliest infancy I gave evidence of having fully inherited the family character. As I advanced in years, it was more strongly developed, becoming for many reasons a cause of serious disquietude to my friends and of positive injury to myself. I grew self-willed, addicted to the wildest caprices, and a prey to the most ungovernable passions. Weak-minded and beset with constitutional infirmities akin to my own, my parents could do but little to check the evil propensities which distinguished me. Some feeble and ill-directed efforts resulted in complete failure on their part and, of course, in total triumph on mine. Thenceforward my voice was a household law, and at an age when few children have abandoned their leading strings, I was left to the guidance of my own will and became, in everything but name, the master of my own actions.

My earliest recollections of a school life are connected with a large, rambling Elizabethan house, in a misty-looking village of England, where were a vast number of gigantic and gnarled trees and where all the houses were excessively ancient. In truth, it was a dreamlike and spirit-soothing place, that venerable old town. At this moment, in fancy, I feel the refreshing chilliness of its deeply shadowed avenues, inhale the fragrance of its thousand shrubberies, and thrill anew with indefinable delight at the deep, hollow note of the church bell, breaking each hour with sullen and sudden roar upon the stillness of the dusky atmosphere in which the fretted Gothic steeple lay embedded and asleep.

It gives me perhaps as much pleasure as I can now in any manner experience to dwell upon minute recollections of the school and its concerns. Steeped in misery as I am—misery, alas! only too real—I shall be pardoned for seeking relief, however slight and temporary, in the weakness of a few rambling details. These, moreover, utterly trivial and even ridiculous in themselves, assume to my fancy adventitious importance, as connected with a period and a locality when and where I recognize the first ambiguous monitions of the destiny which afterward so fully overshadowed me. Let me, then, remember.

The house, I have said, was old and irregular. The grounds were extensive, and a high and solid brick wall, topped with a bed of mortar and broken glass, encompassed the whole. This prisonlike rampart formed the limit of our domain. Beyond it we saw but thrice a week: once every Saturday afternoon, when, attended by two ushers, we were permitted to take brief walks in a body through some of the neighboring fields; and twice during Sunday, when we were paraded in the same formal manner to the morning and evening services in the one church of the village. Of this church the principal of our school was pastor. With how deep a spirit of wonder and perplexity was I wont to regard him, from our remote pew in the gallery, as with step solemn and slow he ascended the pulpit! This reverend man, with countenance so demurely benign, with robes so glossy and so clerically flowing, with wig so minutely powdered, so rigid and so vast —could this be he who, of late, with sour visage and in snuffy habiliments, administered, ferule in hand, the Draconian laws of the academy? O gigantic paradox, too utterly monstrous for solution!

At an angle of the ponderous wall frowned a more ponderous gate. It was riveted and studded with iron bolts and surmounted with jagged iron spikes. What impressions of deep awe did it inspire! It was never opened, save for the three periodical egressions and ingressions already mentioned; then, in every creak of its mighty hinges, we found a plenitude of mystery—a world of matter for solemn remark or for more solemn meditation.

The extensive enclosure was irregular in form, having many capacious recesses. Of these, three or four of the largest constituted the playground. It was level and covered with fine gravel. I well remember it had no trees or benches or anything similar within it. Of course, it was in the rear of the house. In front lay a small parterre, planted with box and other shrubs, but through this sacred division we passed only upon rare occasions indeed, such as a first advent to school or final departure thence or, perhaps, when, a parent or friend having called for us, we joyfully took our way home for the Christmas or midsummer holidays.

But the house! How quaint an old building was this! To me how veritably a palace of enchantment! There was really no end to its windings, to its incomprehensible subdivisions. It was difficult, at any given time, to say with certainty upon which of its two stories one happened to be. From each room to every other, there were sure to be found three or four steps, either in ascent or descent. Then the lateral branches were innumerable, inconceivable, and so returning in upon themselves that our most exact ideas in regard to the whole mansion were not very far different from those with which we pondered upon infinity. During the five years of my residence here, I was never able to ascertain with precision in what remote locality lay the little sleeping apartment assigned to me and some eighteen or twenty other scholars.

The schoolroom was the largest in the house—in the world, I could not help thinking. It was very long, narrow, and dismally low, with pointed Gothic windows and a ceiling of oak. In a remote and terror-inspiring angle was a square enclosure of eight or ten feet, comprising the sanctum, "during hours," of our principal, the Reverend Dr. Bransby. It was a solid structure, with massy door, which, sooner than open in the absence of the "dominie," we would all have willingly perished by the *peine forte et dure.** In other angles were two other similar boxes, far less reverenced, indeed, but still greatly matters of awe. One of these was the pulpit of the "classical" usher and one of the "English and mathematical." Interspersed about the room, crossing and recrossing in endless irregularity, were innumerable benches and desks, black, ancient, and timeworn, piled desperately with much-bethumbed books and so carved with initial letters, names at full length, grotesque figures, and other multiplied efforts of the knife as to have entirely lost what little of original form might have been their portion in days long departed. A huge bucket with water stood at one extremity of the room and a clock of stupendous dimensions at the other.

---

*A form of torture designed to force a prisoner to speak. Weights were applied to the body of the unfortunate captive until he either pleaded or was crushed to death.

Encompassed by the massy walls of this venerable academy, I passed, yet not in tedium or disgust, the years of the third lustrum of my life. The teeming brain of childhood requires no external world of incident to occupy or amuse it, and the apparently dismal monotony of a school was replete with more intense excitement than my riper youth has derived from luxury or my full manhood from crime. Yet I must believe that my first mental development had in it much of the uncommon—even much of the *outré*. Upon mankind at large, the events of very early existence rarely leave in mature age any definite impression. All is gray shadow—a weak and irregular remembrance—an indistinct regathering of feeble pleasures and phantasmagoric pains. With me this is not so. In childhood I must have felt with the energy of a man what I now find stamped upon memory in lines as vivid, as deep, and as durable as the exergues of the Carthaginian medals.

Yet, in fact—in the fact of the world's view—how little there was to remember! The morning's awakening, the nightly summons to bed; the connings, the recitations; the periodical half holidays and perambulations; the playground, with its broils, its pastimes, its intrigues. These, by a mental sorcery long forgotten, were made to involve a wilderness of sensation, a world of rich incident, a universe of varied emotion and excitement most passionate and spirit-stirring. *"Oh, le bon temps, que ce siecle de fer?"**

In truth, the ardor, the enthusiasm, and the imperiousness of my disposition soon rendered me a marked character among my schoolmates and by slow but natural gradations gave me an ascendency over all not greatly older than myself—over all, with a single exception. This exception was found in the person of a scholar who, al-

*"That age of chains, was it truly the good old days?"

though no relation, bore the same Christian name and surname as mine—a circumstance, in fact, little remarkable, for, notwithstanding a noble descent, mine was one of those everyday appellations which seem, by prescriptive right, to have been, time out of mind, the common property of the mob. In this narrative I have therefore designated myself as William Wilson—a fictitious title not very dissimilar to the real. My namesake alone, of those who, in school phraseology, constituted "our set," presumed to compete with me in the studies of the class and in the sports and broils of the playground—to refuse implicit belief in my assertions and submission to my will—indeed, to interfere with my arbitrary dictation in any respect whatsoever. If there is on earth a supreme and unqualified despotism, it is the despotism of a mastermind in boyhood over the less energetic spirits of its unfortunate companions.

Wilson's rebellion was to me a source of the greatest embarrassment, the more so as, in spite of the bravado with which in public I made a point of treating him and his pretensions, I secretly felt that I feared him and could not help thinking the equality which he maintained so easily with me a proof of his true superiority, since not to be overcome cost me a perpetual struggle. Yet this superiority—even this equality—was, in truth, acknowledged by no one but myself; our associates, by some unaccountable blindness, seemed not even to suspect it. Indeed, his competition, his resistance, and especially his impertinent and dogged interference with my purposes were not more pointed than private. He appeared to be destitute alike of the ambition which urged and of the passionate energy of mind which enabled me to excel. In his rivalry, he might have been supposed actuated solely by a whimsical desire to thwart, astonish, or mortify me, although there were times when I could not help observing, with a feeling made up of wonder, abasement, and pique, that he mingled with his injuries, his insults, or his contradictions a certain most inappropriate, and assuredly most unwelcome, *affectionateness* of manner. I could only conceive this singular behavior to arise from a consummate self-conceit assuming the vulgar airs of patronage and protection.

Perhaps it was this latter trait in Wilson's conduct, conjoined with our identity of name and the mere accident of our having entered the school upon the same day, which set afloat the notion that we were brothers among the senior classes in the academy. These do not usually inquire with much strictness into the affairs of their juniors. I have before said, or should have said, that Wilson was not, in the most remote degree, connected with my family. But, assuredly, if we *had* been brothers, we must have been twins, for, after leaving Dr. Bransby's, I casually learned that my namesake was born on the nineteenth of January, 1813—and this is a somewhat remarkable coincidence, for the day is precisely that of my own nativity.

It may seem strange that, in spite of the continual anxiety occasioned me by the rivalry of Wilson and his intolerable spirit of contradiction, I could not bring myself to hate him altogether. We had, to be sure, nearly every day a quarrel, in which, yielding me publicly the palm of victory, he in some manner contrived to make me feel that it was he who had deserved it. Yet a sense of pride on my part and a veritable dignity on his own kept us always upon what are called "speaking terms," while there were many points of strong congeniality in our tempers operating to awake in me a sentiment which our position alone, perhaps, prevented from ripening into friendship.

It is difficult indeed to define or even to describe my real feelings toward him. They formed a motley and heterogeneous admixture: some petulant animosity which was not yet hatred, some esteem, more respect, much fear, and a world of uneasy curiosity. To the moralist it will be unnecessary to say, in addition, that Wilson and I were the most inseparable of companions.

It was no doubt the anomalous state of affairs existing between us which turned all my attacks upon him (and they were many, either open or covert) into the channel of banter or practical joke (giving pain while assuming the aspect of mere fun) rather than into a more serious and determined hostility. But my endeavors on this head were by no means uniformly successful, even when my plans were the most wittily concocted, for my namesake had much about him of that unassuming and quiet austerity which, while enjoying the poignancy of its own jokes, has no heel of Achilles in itself and absolutely refuses to be laughed at. I could find, indeed, but one vulnerable point, and that, lying in a personal peculiarity arising perhaps from constitutional disease, would have been spared by any antagonist less at his wit's end than was I; my rival had a weakness in the faucial, or guttural, organs which precluded him from raising his voice at any time *above a very low whisper*. Of this defect I did not fail to take what poor advantage lay in my power.

Wilson's retaliations in kind were many, and there was one form of his practical wit that disturbed me beyond measure. How his sagacity first discovered at all that so petty a thing would vex me is a question I never could solve, but, having discovered it, he habitually practiced the annoyance. I had always felt aversion to my uncourtly patronymic and its very common, if not plebeian, praenomen. The words were venom in my ears; and when, upon the day of my arrival, a second William Wilson came also to the academy, I felt angry with him for bearing the name and doubly disgusted with the name because a stranger bore it who would be the cause of its twofold repetition, who would be constantly in my presence, and whose concerns, in the ordinary routine of the school business, must inevitably, on account of the detestable coincidence, be often confounded with my own.

The feeling of vexation thus engendered grew stronger with every circumstance tending to show resemblance, moral or physical, between my rival and me. I had not then discovered the remarkable fact that we were of the same age, but I saw that we were of the same height, and I perceived that we were even singularly alike in general contour of person and outline of feature. I was galled, too, by the rumor touching a relationship, which had grown current in the upper forms. In a word, nothing could more seriously disturb me (although I scrupulously concealed such disturbance) than any allusion to a similarity of mind, person, or condition existing between us. But, in truth, I had no reason to believe that (with the exception of the matter of relationship and in the case of Wilson himself) this similarity had ever been made a subject of comment or even observed at all by our schoolfellows. That *he* observed it in all its bearings, and as fixedly as I, was apparent; but that he could discover in such circumstances so fruitful a field of annoyance can only be attributed, as I said before, to his more than ordinary penetration.

His cue, which was to perfect an imitation of me, lay both in words and in actions, and most admirably did he play his part. My dress it was an easy matter to copy; my gait and general manner were without difficulty appropriated; in spite of his constitutional defect, even my voice did not escape him. My louder tones were, of course, unattempted, but the key was identical; *and his singular whisper grew to be the very echo of my own.*

How greatly this most exquisite portraiture harassed me (for it could not justly be termed a caricature) I will not now venture to describe. I had but one consolation—in the fact that the imitation apparently was noticed by me alone and that I had to endure only the knowing and strangely sarcastic smiles of my namesake himself. Satisfied with having produced in my bosom the intended effect, he seemed to chuckle in secret over the sting he had inflicted, characteristically disregardful of the public applause which the success of his witty endeavors might have so easily elicited. That the school, indeed, did not feel his design, perceive its accomplishment, and participate in his sneer was for many anxious months a riddle I could not resolve. Perhaps the *gradation* of his copy rendered it not so readily perceptible, or, more possibly, I owed my security to the masterly aid of the copyist, who, disdaining the letter (which in a painting is all the obtuse can see), gave but the full spirit of his original for my individual contemplation and chagrin.

I have already more than once spoken of the disgusting air of patronage which he assumed toward me and of his frequent officious interference with my will. This interference often took the ungracious character of advice—advice not openly given but hinted or insinuated. I received it with a repugnance which gained strength as I grew in years. Yet, at this distant day, let me do him the simple justice to acknowledge that I can recall no occasion when the suggestions of my rival were on the side of those errors or follies so usual to his immature age and seeming inexperience; that his moral sense, at least, if not his general talents and worldly wisdom, was far keener than my own; and that I might today have been a better, and thus a happier, man had I less frequently rejected the counsels embodied in those meaning whispers which I then but too cordially hated and too bitterly despised.

As it was, I at length grew restive in the extreme under his distasteful supervision and daily resented more and more openly what I considered his intolerable arrogance. I have said that in the first years of our connection as schoolmates my feelings in regard to him might have been easily ripened into friendship; but in the latter months of my residence at the academy, although the intrusion of his ordinary manner had, beyond doubt, in some measure abated, my sentiments, in nearly similar proportion, partook very much of positive hatred. Upon one occasion he saw this, I think, and afterward avoided, or made a show of avoiding, me.

It was about the same period, if I remember aright, that, in an altercation of violence with him, in which he was more than usually thrown off his guard and spoke and acted with an openness of demeanor rather foreign to his nature, I discovered, or fancied I discovered, in his accent, his air, and general appearance a something which first startled and then deeply interested me, by bringing to mind dim visions of my earliest infancy—wild, confused, and thronging memories of a time when memory herself was yet unborn. I cannot better describe the sensation which oppressed me than by saying that I could with difficulty shake off the belief of my having been acquainted with the being who stood before me at some epoch very long ago, some point of the past even infinitely remote. The delusion, however, faded as rapidly as it came, and I mention it at all but to define the day of the last conversation I held there with my singular namesake.

The huge old house, with its countless subdivisions, had

several large chambers communicating with each other, where slept the greater number of students. There were, however (as must necessarily happen in a building so awkwardly planned), many little nooks or recesses, the odds and ends of the structure, and these the economic ingenuity of Dr. Bransby had also fitted up as dormitories, although, being the merest closets, they were capable of accommodating but a single individual. One of these small apartments was occupied by Wilson.

One night, about the close of my fifth year at the school and immediately after the altercation just mentioned, finding everyone wrapped in sleep, I arose from bed and, lamp in hand, stole through a wilderness of narrow passages from my own bedroom to that of my rival. I had long been plotting one of those ill-natured pieces of practical wit at his expense, in which I had hitherto been so uniformly unsuccessful. It was my intention now to put my scheme in operation, and I resolved to make him feel the whole extent of the malice with which I was imbued. Having reached his closet, I noiselessly entered, leaving the lamp, with a shade over it, on the outside. I advanced a step and listened to the sound of his tranquil breathing. Assured of his being asleep, I returned, took the light, and with it again approached the bed. Close curtains were around it, which, in the prosecution of my plan, I slowly and quietly withdrew, when the bright rays fell vividly upon the sleeper, and my eyes, at the same moment, fell upon his countenance. I looked, and a numbness, an iciness of feeling, instantly pervaded my frame. My breast heaved, my knees tottered, my whole spirit became possessed with an objectless yet intolerable horror. Gasping for breath, I lowered the lamp in still nearer proximity to the face. Were these—*these*—the lineaments of William Wilson? I saw, indeed, that they were his, but I shook as if with a fit of the ague in fancying they were not. What *was* there about them to confound me in this manner? I gazed, while my brain reeled with a multitude of incoherent thoughts. Not thus he appeared, assuredly not *thus*, in the vivacity of his waking hours. The same name, the same contour of person, the same day of arrival at the academy; and then his dogged and meaningless imitation of my gait, my voice, my habits, and my manner. Was it, in truth, within the bounds of human possibility that *what I now saw* was the result merely of the habitual practice of this sarcastic imitation? Awestricken and with a creeping shudder, I extinguished the lamp, passed silently from the chamber, and left at once the halls of that old academy, never to enter them again.

After a lapse of some months, spent at home in mere idleness, I found myself a student at Eton. The brief interval had been sufficient to enfeeble my remembrance of the events at Dr. Bransby's or at least to effect a material change in the nature of the feelings with which I remembered them. The truth, the tragedy, of the drama was no more. I could now find room to doubt the evidence of my senses and seldom called up the subject at all but with wonder at the extent of human credulity and a smile at the vivid force of the imagination which I hereditarily possessed. Neither was this species of skepticism likely to be diminished by the character of the life I led at Eton. The vortex of thoughtless folly into which I there so immediately and so recklessly plunged washed away all but the froth of my past hours, engulfed at once every solid or serious impression, and left to memory only the veriest levities of a former existence.

I do not wish, however, to trace the course of my miserable profligacy here—a profligacy which set at defiance the laws, while it eluded the vigilance of the institution.

Three years of folly, passed without profit, had but given me rooted habits of vice and added, to a somewhat unusual degree, to my bodily stature, when, after a week of soulless dissipation, I invited a small party of the most dissolute students to a secret carousal in my chambers. We met at a late hour of the night, for our debaucheries were to be faithfully protracted until morning. The wine flowed freely, and there were not wanting other and perhaps more dangerous seductions, so that the gray dawn had already faintly appeared in the east while our delirious extravagance was at its height. Madly flushed with cards and intoxication, I was in the act of insisting upon a toast of more than wonted profanity, when my attention was suddenly diverted by the violent, although partial, unclosing of the door of the apartment and by the eager voice of a servant from without. He said that some person, apparently in great haste, demanded to speak with me in the hall.

As I was wildly excited with wine, the unexpected interruption rather delighted than surprised me. I staggered forward at once, and a few steps brought me to the vestibule of the building. In this low and small room there hung no lamp, and now no light at all was admitted, save that of the exceedingly feeble dawn which made its way through the semicircular window. As I put my foot over the threshold, I became aware of the figure of a youth about my own height, habited in a white kerseymere morning frock cut in the novel fashion of the one I myself wore at the moment. This the faint light enabled me to perceive, but the features of his face I could not distinguish. Upon my entering, he strode hurriedly up to me and, seizing me by the arm with a gesture of petulant impatience, whispered, "William Wilson!" in my ear.

I grew perfectly sober in an instant.

There was that in the manner of the stranger, and in the tremulous shake of his uplifted finger as he held it between my eyes and the light, which filled me with unqualified amazement; but it was not this which had so violently moved me. It was the pregnancy of solemn admonition in the singular low, hissing utterance, and, above all, it was the character, the tone, *the key,* of those few simple and familiar, yet *whispered,* syllables which came with a thousand thronging memories of bygone days and struck upon my soul with the shock of a galvanic battery. Ere I could recover the use of my senses, he was gone.

Although this event failed not of a vivid effect upon my disordered imagination, yet was it as evanescent as vivid. For some weeks, indeed, I busied myself in earnest inquiry or was wrapped in a cloud of morbid speculation. I did not pretend to disguise from my perception the identity of the singular individual who thus perseveringly interfered with my affairs and harassed me with his insinuated counsel. But who and what was this Wilson?—and whence came he?—and what were his purposes? Upon none of these points could I be satisfied, merely ascertaining, in regard to him, that a sudden accident in his family had caused his removal from Dr. Bransby's academy on the afternoon of the day in which I myself had eloped. But in a brief period I ceased to think upon the subject, my attention being all absorbed in a contemplated departure for Oxford. Thither I soon went, the incalculating vanity of my parents furnishing me with an outfit and annual establishment which would enable me to indulge at will in the luxury already so dear to my heart—to vie in profuseness of expenditure with the haughtiest heirs of the wealthiest earldoms in Great Britain.

Excited by such appliances to vice, my constitutional

temperament broke forth with redoubled ardor, and I spurned even the common restraints of decency in the mad infatuation of my revels. But it is absurd to pause in the detail of my extravagance. Let it suffice that among spendthrifts I out-Heroded Herod and that, giving name to a multitude of novel follies, I added no brief appendix to the long catalog of vices then usual in the most dissolute university of Europe.

It could hardly be credited, however, that I had, even here, so utterly fallen from the gentlemanly estate as to seek acquaintance with the vilest arts of the gambler by profession, and, having become an adept in his despicable science, I practiced it habitually as a means of increasing my already enormous income at the expense of the weak-minded among my fellow collegians. Such, nevertheless, was the fact; and the very enormity of this offense against all manly and honorable sentiment proved, beyond doubt, the main, if not the sole, reason for the impunity with which it was committed. Who, indeed, among my most abandoned associates would not rather have disputed the clearest evidence of his senses than have suspected of such courses the gay, the frank, the generous William Wilson—the noblest and most liberal commoner at Oxford—him whose follies (said his parasites) were but the follies of youth and unbridled fancy—whose errors but inimitable whim—whose darkest vice but a careless and dashing extravagance?

I had been for two years successfully busied in this way, when there came to the university a young parvenu nobleman, Glendinning—as rich, said report, as Herodes Atticus; his riches, too, as easily acquired. I soon found him of weak intellect and, of course, marked him as a fitting subject for my skill. I frequently engaged him in play and contrived, with the gambler's usual art, to let him win considerable sums, the more effectually to entangle him in my snares. At length, my schemes being ripe, I met him (with the full intention that this meeting should be final and decisive) at the chambers of a fellow commoner (Mr. Preston), who was equally intimate with us both, but who, to do him justice, entertained not even a remote suspicion of my design. To give to this a better coloring, I had contrived to have assembled a party of some eight or ten and was solicitously careful that the introduction of cards should appear accidental and originate in the proposal of my contemplated dupe himself. To be brief upon a vile topic, none of the low finesse so customary upon similar occasions that it is a just matter for wonder how any are still found so besotted as to fall its victim was omitted.

We had protracted our sitting far into the night, and I had at length effected the maneuver of getting Glendinning as my sole antagonist. The game, too, was my favorite, écarté. The rest of the company, interested in the extent of our play, had abandoned their own cards and were standing around us as spectators. The parvenu, who had been induced by my artifices in the early part of the evening to drink deeply, now shuffled, dealt, and played with a wild nervousness of manner for which his intoxication, I thought, might partially but could not altogether account. In a very short period, he had become my debtor to a large amount; then, having taken a long draft of port, he did precisely what I had been coolly anticipating—he proposed to double our already extravagant stakes. With a well-feigned show of reluctance and not until after my repeated refusal had seduced him into some angry words, which gave a color of pique to my compliance, did I finally comply. The result, of course, did but prove how entirely the prey was in my toils: In less than an hour he had quadrupled his debt. For some time his countenance had been losing the florid tinge lent it by the wine, but now, to my astonishment, I perceived that it had grown to a pallor truly fearful. I say to my astonishment. Glendinning had been represented to my eager inquiries as immeasurably wealthy, and the sums which he had as yet lost, although in themselves vast, could not, I supposed, very seriously annoy, much less so violently affect, him. That he was overcome by the wine just swallowed was the idea which most readily presented itself; and rather with a view to the preservation of my own character in the eyes of my associates than from any less interested motive, I was about to insist peremptorily upon a discontinuance of the play, when some expressions at my elbow from among the company and an ejaculation evincing utter despair on the part of Glendinning gave me to understand that I had effected his total ruin, under circumstances which, rendering him an object for the pity of all, should have protected him from the ill offices even of a fiend.

What now might have been my conduct, it is difficult to say. The pitiable condition of my dupe had thrown an air of embarrassed gloom over all, and for some moments a profound silence was maintained, during which I could not help feeling my cheeks tingle with the many burning glances of scorn or reproach cast upon me by the less abandoned of the party. I will even own that an intolerable weight of anxiety was for a brief instant lifted from my bosom by the sudden and extraordinary interruption which ensued. The wide, heavy folding doors of the apartment were all at once thrown open to their full extent, with a vigorous and rushing impetuosity that extinguished, as if by magic, every candle in the room. Their light, in dying, enabled us just to perceive that a stranger had entered, about my own height and closely muffled in a cloak. The darkness, however, was now total, and we could only *feel* that he was standing in our midst. Before any one of us could recover from the extreme astonishment into which this rudeness had thrown all, we heard the voice of the intruder.

"Gentlemen," he said in a low, distinct, and never-to-be-forgotten *whisper* which thrilled to the very marrow of my bones. "Gentlemen, I make no apology for this behavior, because in thus behaving I am but fulfilling my duty. You are, beyond doubt, uninformed of the true character of the person who has tonight won at écarté a large sum of money from Lord Glendinning. I will therefore put you upon an expeditious and decisive plan of obtaining this very necessary information. Please to examine, at your leisure, the inner linings of the cuff of his left sleeve and the several little packages which may be found in the somewhat capacious pockets of his embroidered morning wrapper."

While he spoke, so profound was the stillness that one might have heard a pin drop upon the floor. In ceasing, he departed at once, as abruptly as he had entered. Can I—shall I—describe my sensations? Must I say that I felt all the horrors of the damned? Most assuredly I had little time for reflection. Many hands roughly seized me upon the spot, and lights were immediately reprocured. A search ensued. In the lining of my sleeve were found all the court cards essential in écarté, and in the pockets of my wrapper a number of packs, facsimiles of those used at our sittings, with the single exception that mine were of the species called, technically, *arrondées,* the honors being slightly convex at the ends, the lower cards slightly convex at the sides. In this disposition, the dupe who cuts, as customary, at the length of the pack will invariably find that he cuts his antagonist an honor, while the gambler, cutting at the breadth, will as certainly cut nothing for his victim which may count in the records of the game.

Any burst of indignation upon this discovery would have affected me less than the silent contempt and the sarcastic composure with which it was received.

"Mr. Wilson—" said our host, stooping to remove from beneath his feet an exceedingly luxurious cloak of rare furs—"Mr. Wilson, this is your property." (The weather was cold, and, upon quitting my own room, I had thrown a cloak over my dressing wrapper, putting it off upon reaching the scene of play.) "I presume it is supererogatory to seek here" (eyeing the folds of the garment with a bitter smile) "for any further evidence of your skill. Indeed, we have had enough. You will see the necessity, I hope, of quitting Oxford—at all events, of quitting instantly my chambers."

Abased, humbled to the dust as I then was, it is probable that I should have resented this galling language by immediate personal violence had not my whole attention been at the moment arrested by a fact of the most startling character. The cloak which I had worn was of a rare description of fur; how rare, how extravagantly costly, I shall not venture to say. Its fashion, too, was of my own fantastic invention, for I was fastidious to an absurd degree of coxcombry in matters of this frivolous nature. When, therefore, Mr. Preston reached me the cloak which he had picked up from the floor near the folding doors of the apartment, it was with an astonishment nearly bordering upon terror that I perceived that my own was already hanging on my arm (where I had, no doubt, unwittingly placed it) and that the one presented me was but its exact counterpart in every, in even the minutest possible, particular. The singular being who had so disastrously exposed me had been muffled, I remembered, in a cloak, and none had been worn at all by any of the members of our party with the exception of me. Retaining some presence of mind, I took the one offered me by Preston, placed it unnoticed over my own, left the apartment with a resolute scowl of defiance, and next morning, ere dawn of day, commenced a hurried journey from Oxford to the Continent, in a perfect agony of horror and of shame.

I fled in vain. My evil destiny pursued me, as if in exultation, and proved indeed that the exercise of its mysterious dominion had as yet only begun. Scarcely had I set foot in Paris ere I had fresh evidence of the detestable interest taken by this Wilson in my concerns. Years flew, while I experienced no relief. Villain! At Rome, with how untimely, yet with how spectral, an officiousness, stepped he in between me and my ambition! At Vienna, too—at Berlin—and at Moscow! Where, in truth, had I *not* bitter cause to curse him within my heart? From his inscrutable tyranny did I at length flee, panic-stricken, as from a pestilence; and to the very ends of the earth, *I fled in vain.*

And again and again, in secret communion with my own spirit, would I demand the questions, "Who is he? Whence came he? And what are his objects?" But no answer was there found. And now I scrutinized, with a minute scrutiny, the forms and the methods and the leading traits of his impertinent supervision. But even here there was very little upon which to base a conjecture. It was noticeable, indeed, that in no one of the multiplied instances in which he had of late crossed my path had he crossed it except to frustrate those schemes or to disturb those actions which, if fully carried out, might have resulted in bitter mischief. Poor justification this, in truth, for an authority so imperiously assumed! Poor indemnity for natural rights of self-agency so pertinaciously denied!

I had also been forced to notice that my tormentor, for a very long period of time (while scrupulously and with miraculous dexterity maintaining his whim of an identity of apparel with myself), had so contrived it, in the execution of his varied interference with my will, that I saw not at any moment the features of his face. Be Wilson what he might, *this,* at least, was but the veriest of affectation or of folly. Could he for an instant have supposed that in my admonisher at Eton—in the destroyer of my honor at Oxford—in him who thwarted my ambition at Rome, my revenge at Paris, my passionate love at Naples, or what he falsely termed my avarice in Egypt—that in this, my archenemy and evil genius, I could fail to recognize the William Wilson of my schoolboy days—the namesake, the companion, the rival—the hated and dreaded rival at Dr. Bransby's? Impossible! But let me hasten to the last eventful scene of the drama.

Thus far I had succumbed supinely to this imperious domination. The sentiment of deep awe with which I habitually regarded the elevated character, the majestic wisdom, the apparent omnipresence, and the omnipotence of Wilson, added to a feeling of even terror with which certain other traits in his nature and assumptions inspired me, had operated hitherto to impress me with an idea of my own utter weakness and helplessness and to suggest an implicit, although bitterly reluctant, submission to his arbitrary will. But of late days I had given myself up entirely to wine, and its maddening influence upon my hereditary temper rendered me more and more impatient of control. I began to murmur—to hesitate—to resist. And was it only fancy which induced me to believe that with the increase of my own firmness, that of my tormentor underwent a proportional diminution? Be this as it may, I now began to feel the inspiration of a burning hope and at length nurtured in my secret thoughts a stern and desperate resolution that I would submit no longer to be enslaved.

It was at Rome, during the Carnival of 18—, that I attended a masquerade in the *palazzo* of the Neapolitan Duke di Broglio. I had indulged more freely than usual in the excesses of the wine table, and now the suffocating atmosphere of the crowded rooms irritated me beyond endurance. The difficulty, too, of forcing my way through the mazes of the company contributed not a little to the ruffling of my temper, for I was anxiously seeking (let me not say with what unworthy motive) the young, the gay, the beautiful wife of the aged and doting Di Broglio. With a too unscrupulous confidence, she had previously communicated to me the secret of the costume in which she would be habited, and now, having caught a glimpse of her person, I was hurrying to make my way into her presence. At this moment I felt a light hand placed upon my shoulder and that ever remembered low, damnable *whisper* within my ear.

In an absolute frenzy of wrath, I turned at once upon him who had thus interrupted me and seized him violently by the collar. He was attired, as I had expected, in a costume altogether similar to my own, wearing a Spanish cloak of blue velvet, begirt about the waist with a crimson belt sustaining a rapier. A mask of black silk entirely covered his face.

"Scoundrel!" I said, in a voice husky with rage, while every syllable I uttered seemed as new fuel to my fury. "Scoundrel! Impostor! Accursed villain! You shall not—you *shall not* dog me unto death! Follow me, or I stab you where you stand!" And I broke my way from the ballroom into a small antechamber adjoining, dragging him unresistingly with me as I went.

Upon entering, I thrust him furiously from me. He staggered against the wall, while I closed the door with an oath and commanded him to draw. He hesitated but for an instant, then, with a slight sigh, drew in silence and put himself upon his defense.

The contest was brief indeed. I was frantic with every species of wild excitement and felt within my single arm the energy and power of a multitude. In a few seconds I forced him, by sheer strength, against the wainscoting and thus, getting him at mercy, plunged my sword, with brute ferocity, repeatedly through and through his bosom.

At that instant some person tried the latch of the door. I hastened to prevent an intrusion and then immediately returned to my dying antagonist. But what human language can adequately portray *that* astonishment, *that* horror, which possessed me at the spectacle then presented to view? The brief moment in which I averted my eyes had been sufficient to produce, apparently, a material change in the arrangements at the upper, or farther, end of the room. A large mirror—so at first it seemed to me, in my confusion—now stood where none had been perceptible before; and as I stepped up to it in extremity of terror, mine own image, but with features all pale and dabbled in blood, advanced to meet me with a feeble and tottering gait.

Thus it appeared, I say, but was not. It was my antagonist—it was Wilson who then stood before me in the agonies of his dissolution. His mask and cloak lay where he had thrown them upon the floor. Not a thread in all his raiment—not a line in all the marked and singular lineaments of his face—which was not, even in the most absolute identity, *mine own!*

It was Wilson; but he spoke no longer in a whisper,

and I could have fancied that I myself was speaking while he said:

"*You have conquered, and I yield. Yet, henceforward, art thou also dead—dead to the World, to Heaven, and to Hope! In me didst thou exist—and, in my death, see by this image, which is thine own, how utterly thou hast murdered thyself.*"

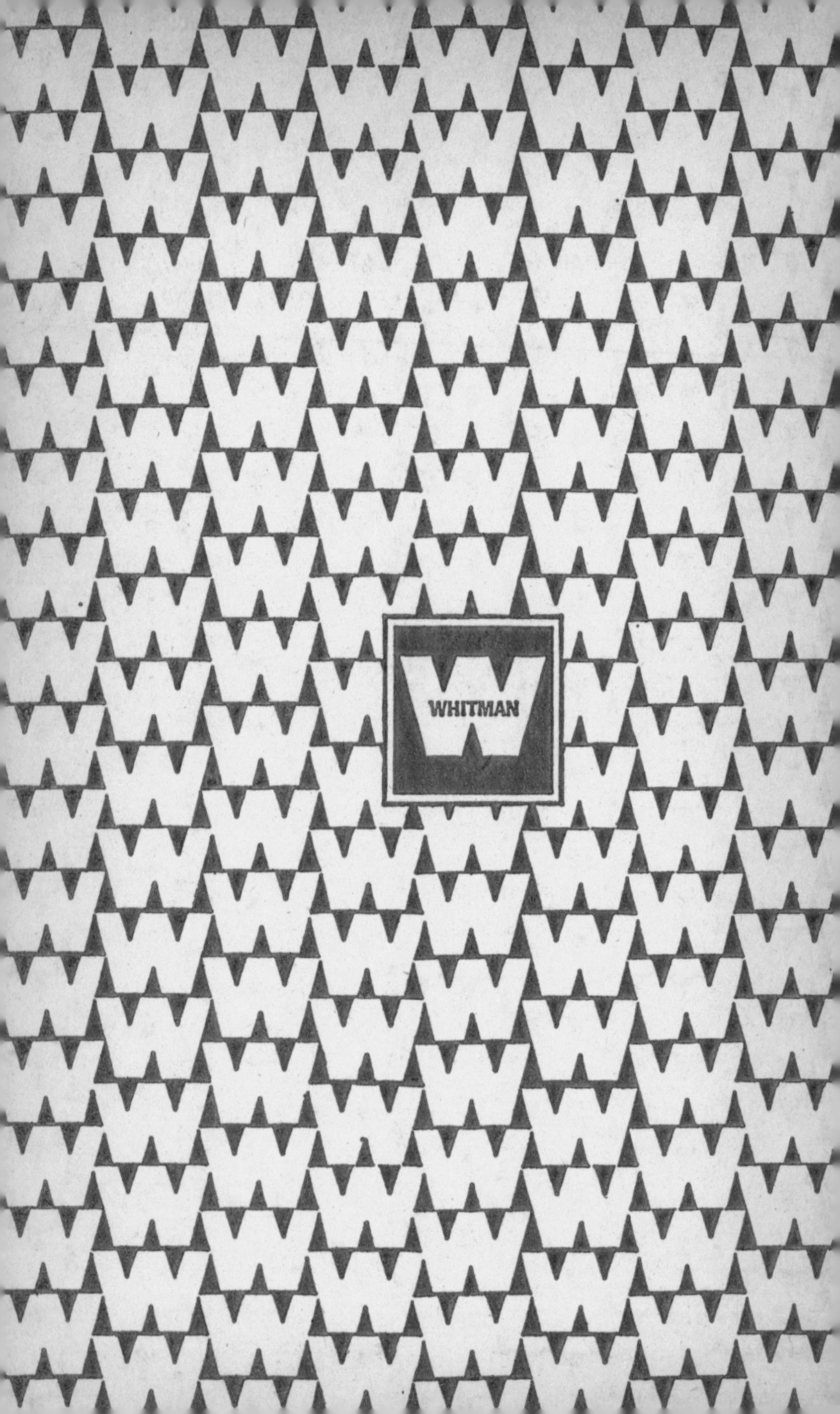
WHITMAN